Her greatest weakness was her son's safety. If the kidnappers threatened to hurt him, she knew she'd go along with whatever they asked of her.

Rachel turned to walk away, but suddenly Nick grabbed her hand to stop her. Glancing over her shoulder, she found him staring at her intently. "What's wrong?" she asked.

"Nothing. Just—be careful, okay?" he said gruffly. Then, before she could respond, he pulled her close and gave her a quick kiss.

The kiss was over before she had a chance to register what had happened. But she longed to throw herself into his arms, absorbing some of his strength. This wasn't the time or the place, though, so she said the first thing that came to mind. "Remember your promise," she blurted. "No matter what happens, save my son."

Books by Laura Scott

Love Inspired Suspense

The Thanksgiving Target
Secret Agent Father
The Christmas Rescue
Lawman-in-Charge
Proof of Life
Identity Crisis
Twin Peril
Undercover Cowboy
Her Mistletoe Protector

LAURA SCOTT

grew up reading faith-based romance books by Grace Livingston Hill, but as much as she loved the stories, she longed for a bit more mystery and suspense. She is honored to write for the Love Inspired Suspense line, where a reader can find a heartwarming journey of faith amid the thrilling danger.

Laura lives with her husband of twenty-five years and has two children, a daughter and a son, who are both in college. She works as a critical-care nurse during the day at a large level-one trauma center in Milwaukee, Wisconsin, and spends her spare time writing romance.

Please visit Laura at www.laurascottbooks.com, as she loves to hear from her readers.

HER MISTLETOE
PROTECTOR

LAURA SCOTT

HARLEQUIN® LOVE INSPIRED® SUSPENSE

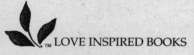

LOVE INSPIRED BOOKS

ISBN-13: 978-0-373-44562-2

HER MISTLETOE PROTECTOR

www.Harlequin.com

Rejoice in the Lord always.
I will say it again: Rejoice!
—*Philippians* 4:4

This book is dedicated to my sister Michele Glynn.
I know Madison is only an hour away,
but I still miss you so much. I love you!

ONE

"Ms. Simon, wait! I have a letter for you."

Rachel Simon, CEO of Simon Inc., froze, despite the fact that she was running late for her nine-o'clock meeting. The sick feeling in her stomach swelled with dread as she forced herself to turn and face the receptionist.

"Here you go," Carrie Freeman said with a wide smile.

Rachel stared at the thin envelope with her name typed neatly on the front, the dread congealing into a mass of fear. The letter looked exactly like the one she'd received in her mailbox at home last night, and she instinctively knew there was another threat inside. She swallowed hard and took the envelope from the receptionist, being careful to hold it along the edges. Then she cleared her throat. "Who dropped this off for me, Carrie?"

"I don't know… It was sitting on my desk chair when I came back from the restroom. There was a sticky note, telling me to deliver it to you first thing."

Rachel tried hard to keep her fear from showing as she cast a worried gaze around the lobby. Was the person who had left the note watching her right now? "Do you still have the sticky note?" she asked.

Carrie's expression turned perplexed. "I tossed it in the trash bin." Rachel glanced over the receptionist's shoulder at the large stainless-steel trash container standing near the lobby door. "Do you want me to go through the garbage to find it?" Carrie's tone indicated she wasn't thrilled with the idea of pawing in the trash although Rachel knew she would if asked.

As much as she wanted to see the note, she shook her head. Asking Carrie to search through the bin would only bring unwanted attention to herself. She wasn't ready to go public with the weird phone calls and the threatening letter she'd received. The last thing she needed was some sort of leak to the media, as if her company hadn't been through the wringer already.

"No thanks, just curious to see if I recognized the handwriting, that's all. Thanks again, Carrie."

Rachel turned back toward the elevators, her mind focused on the contents of the letter rather than on her upcoming meeting with the two top research scientists in her pharmaceutical company.

The ride to the tenth floor, where her office suite was located, seemed to take forever. She smiled and chatted with various employees as if the envelope in her hand didn't matter.

"Good morning, Rachel," her senior administrative assistant, Edith Goodman, said as she entered through the glass doors. "Dr. Gardener and Dr. Errol are waiting for you in the conference room."

"I'm sorry, but please tell Josie and Karl that I'll need to reschedule our meeting."

Surprise flashed in Edith's eyes, but she quickly nodded and crossed over to the conference room next to Rachel's office. As her assistant delivered the news to the two researchers, Rachel ducked inside her office and closed the door, dropping the envelope on her desk as if it might burn her fingers.

She didn't have any gloves, so she put another piece of paper over the envelope and used her letter opener to slice beneath the flap. Inside was a single piece of paper with a computer-printed message, exactly like the one she'd received at home. Her stomach knotted with anxiety as she carefully opened the paper and read the short message.

"You will scream in agony, suffering for your past mistakes."

She shivered, the words searing into her mind. She opened her purse and drew out the letter she'd received last night, when she and her son, Joey, had come home from basketball practice. The wording was similar, yet different.

"You will repay your debt of betrayal."

The two letters, spread out side by side on her desk, seemed to mock her. She couldn't ignore the threat any longer, not when she knew, with grim certainty, the source of the veiled threat.

The only person she'd ever betrayed was her ex-husband, former State Senator Anthony Caruso. A few months after they were married, the joy of discovering she was pregnant was marred by learning Anthony had ties to organized crime. At first she couldn't believe he was involved in anything illegal. She was embarrassed that the man she'd fallen in love with was nothing more than an illusion. His fake charm covered a black soul.

All too soon, Anthony was openly talking about his Mafia association as if nothing she did could touch him.

But he'd been wrong. She'd lived in fear for months, but one night, he'd lost control and hit her hard enough to give her a black eye and a minor concussion. The evidence of physical abuse, along with her father's money—and the fact that her father's best friend was a judge—helped her buy her freedom.

And Joey's, too. She received sole custody of their son and a no-contact order. Joey was nine years old now, and she was eternally grateful Anthony hadn't seen his son since Joey's first birthday.

But since Anthony's untimely death last year during a crime bust, it was obvious he couldn't have sent these letters. So who had? She could only assume they'd come from someone inside the Chicago Mafia. Most likely from Anthony's uncle, Frankie Caruso.

She buried her face in her hands and fought the rising wave of helplessness. How long would she continue to pay for her naive mistake of marrying Anthony? This past year, since her ex-husband's death, she'd thought she was finally safe. But now it seemed the Mafia wasn't going to leave her alone.

Ever.

Taking several deep breaths, she did her best to control her fear. When she raised her head, she knew she had to take action. With trembling fingers, she went through her files to find the business card of a Chicago police detective who'd questioned her about Anthony last year. She needed to talk to someone who knew the truth about Anthony. Someone who understood how deeply infiltrated the Mafia was in this city.

Someone who would believe her—like Detective Nick Butler. They'd only met a few times, but she remembered him well. He was tall, broad shouldered with light brown hair and amazing blue eyes. In so many ways, Nick was the complete opposite of her ex-husband.

To be honest, Detective Butler hadn't been very happy with her last year during his investigation of Anthony, but that knowledge wasn't enough to stop her from picking up her phone and making the call.

If there was one thing she knew about Detective Butler,

it was that he sincerely cared about justice. He'd worked against the Mafia before. She could only hope that he wouldn't turn his back on her now.

Nick stared at the various reports spread over his desk as he tried to figure out a way to breathe new life into his dead-end cases. With his partner out on medical leave and the upcoming holidays, he hadn't been assigned anything new. But working their old cases felt pretty much like beating his head against a brick wall.

When his phone rang, he answered it absently. "Detective Butler."

"Good morning, Detective. I don't know if you remember me, but my name is Rachel Simon."

Nick straightened in his chair, his instincts on full alert. "Of course, I remember you, Ms. Simon. How are you and your son, Joey, doing?"

"Fine. Well, sort of fine. I, uh, have a problem I'd like to discuss with you. I think it's linked to your past investigation…."

The subtle reference to the Mafia wasn't lost on him. He was surprised to hear from Rachel after all this time, yet he couldn't ignore the underlying hint of fear in her tone. He rose to his feet and glanced at his watch. "I can meet you now, if that works."

"That would be great. Do you remember where my office is located?"

"Yes. I can be there in fifteen minutes."

"Thank you."

After ending the call, Nick slid his cell phone into his pocket and strode to the door. He remembered Rachel Simon very well, as he'd questioned her last year related to a missing-person's case. Her ex-husband had been the prime suspect in the twenty-two-year-old model's disappearance.

Rachel hadn't been much help to his investigation, because she claimed she hadn't seen or spoken to her husband in seven years. Which, based on the divorce settlement and the no-contact order he'd uncovered, was likely true. But at the time he'd felt certain she was holding back on him, that she knew far more about her ex-husband's connection to the Mafia than she'd let on. And even then, her fear of her ex had been palpable.

Ironic how she'd contacted him now that she needed his assistance. And he couldn't deny being curious as to what was going on.

The ride to the office building of Simon Inc. took less than his allotted fifteen minutes. He walked into the lobby and smiled at the perky redhead sitting behind the receptionist desk. "Good morning, I'm here to see Ms. Simon."

"Yes, she mentioned you were coming." The redhead wore a name tag that identified her as Carrie Freeman and she was young enough to make him feel ancient at thirty-seven. "Just take these elevators here to the tenth floor."

"Thanks." He pushed the elevator button, already knowing Rachel's office was on the tenth floor. Once he arrived up there, he was greeted warmly by Rachel's assistant, Edith Goodman. A far cry from the last time he'd been here, when the sixty-something-year-old had protected her boss like a mama bear hovering over her cub.

"Rachel's waiting for you in her office," Edith said. "Is there something I can get for you, Detective? Coffee? Soft drink?"

"Coffee would be great."

"Black, no sugar, correct?"

He shouldn't have been surprised she remembered,

considering Edith Goodman ruled Rachel's office with an iron fist. "That's right."

Rachel's office door was open, and she met him halfway, offering her hand as he strolled toward her. "Detective, thanks for coming on such short notice."

Her slender fingers were firm as they gripped his. She was as beautiful as he remembered, with her sleek blond hair framing her face and distinctive green eyes. But despite her smile, dark shadows hovered in her eyes. "I have to admit, I was intrigued by your call."

Her smile faded, and she waited until Edith had handed him a mug of coffee, before inviting him inside her office. "Please, have a seat."

He sat in the chair facing hers, and his gaze immediately landed on the two pieces of paper lying on her desk. They'd been turned toward him. He took a sip from the steaming mug before setting his coffee aside. He leaned forward and read the messages.

"You will repay your debt of betrayal."

"You will scream in agony, suffering for your past mistakes."

The threats were all too real and his protective instincts jumped to the forefront. He was angry at the idea of Rachel being stalked by some lunatic. He lifted his gaze to meet hers. "Who sent these to you?" he demanded roughly.

"Isn't it obvious?" Rachel scowled and crossed her arms protectively across her chest.

"Not to me," he said, striving for patience. "An exboyfriend? A disgruntled employee? You must have some idea."

Her scowl deepened. "I don't have a boyfriend, ex or otherwise, and a disgruntled employee would more likely try to sue me rather than send threats. I've received a few phone calls, too. The caller never speaks, but I can hear heavy breathing on the other end of the phone. Don't you see?" She spread her hands over the letters. "These have to be from someone within the Mafia."

He stared at her for a long moment, trying to figure out what was going on in her mind. Their last interaction hadn't been entirely cordial, since she'd avoided discussing anything related to her husband's ties to the Mafia. He sat back and reached for his coffee mug. "So you're admitting that Anthony Caruso was involved with the Mafia?"

Her cheeks turned pink and she avoided his gaze as if embarrassed. "I told you that much a year ago," she said defensively.

"But you claimed you didn't know any details," he reminded her.

"Look, Detective, my goal last year was to do whatever was necessary to protect my son. And I never lied to you about that missing woman. At the time we spoke I hadn't seen Anthony in seven years, so I had no idea who he was seeing or who he was associating with."

"But you knew what he was capable of," Nick said, capturing her gaze with his.

She stared at him for a long moment before breaking the connection. And when she spoke, her voice was so soft he could barely hear her. "Yes. I knew exactly what he was capable of. I believe he murdered that woman. But my belief is a far cry from actual hard-core evidence. There was nothing that I knew that would have helped your case."

The simple admission helped squelch his lingering anger. He was a bit ashamed that he'd spent time rehashing the past instead of moving forward. He caught sight of the photo of her son, Joey, that was displayed proudly on her desk. The kid had blond hair, green eyes and a smile that matched his mother's. Nick could understand her need to keep silent if it meant protecting her child.

For a moment, he thought about how much he missed his wife and daughter. He would have done anything to protect them, too. But unfortunately, they both died in a terrible car accident two years ago. And while he knew they were in a much better place in heaven, he still missed them every day.

He pushed the painful memories aside. "Okay, maybe someone within the Mafia sent them, but at this point, we don't have any proof. We can't go after anyone in the syndicate without evidence. I'll take these notes and have them dusted for prints. Maybe that'll give us a place to start."

She grimaced. "Well, to be perfectly honest, the first one probably won't help much. I treated it normally since I had no idea that it was a threat. The second letter I was very careful with, although the envelope was handled by my receptionist." She went on to describe in detail how she'd received the letters.

He made notes in his notebook. "Do you remember when the phone calls came in?" he asked. "Was there a common number?"

"The calls came from a blocked number, and they started three days ago."

Three phone calls and two written threats in the past three days. Hard to tell if the danger was escalating. He'd known some stalkers who called their victims twenty or thirty times a day. These messages seemed to be aimed at keeping Rachel off balance and afraid. "You haven't noticed anyone following you? Or watching you?"

"No. Nothing like that." Her gaze rested on her son's photograph. "Right now, the threats are centered on me, but I called you because I need to be sure Joey is safe."

"I understand. I'll see what we can get from these letters, but at this point, our hands are tied." As much as he wanted to order protection for her, they needed more than just her suspicion that the Mafia was behind the threats. He took out his business card and slid it across the desk. "I want you to be extra vigilant. If you see anything suspicious, please call me on my personal phone regardless of the time of day or night."

She took the card and nodded. "Thank you."

He rose to his feet, wishing there was more that could be done. After donning a pair of gloves, he placed both notes and the envelopes in a plastic evidence bag, even though he knew the odds of getting a decent set of prints were slim. And they'd have to get Rachel's fingerprints as well as the receptionist's on file to cross match them.

Having a new case to work on would help keep him busy. But first he needed to see what the forensic team came up with. Otherwise, he'd have nothing to go on, which wouldn't help keep Rachel and her son safe.

And he wasn't about to lose another mother and child on his watch.

Rachel managed to get some work done before heading out to take Joey to his last basketball game before the Christmas holiday. The drive to the school, located on the outskirts of town, was uneventful. The game turned out to be a lot of fun and her son scored four points, edging their team to a ten to eight victory. Joey and his teammates were loud and rambunctious as they celebrated, and Rachel felt more at ease as the night unfolded. But as she and Joey headed home, she noticed a big black truck keeping pace behind her. No matter what speed she chose to go, the truck remained right behind her.

Detective Butler had warned her to be on the lookout

for anything suspicious. At the moment, the truck certainly seemed suspicious, but maybe she was letting her imagination get the better of her. She didn't recall seeing a truck behind her on the way to the basketball game or parked anywhere along the long country road outside the school.

So how would the driver of the black truck know where to find her? How would anyone have access to Joey's basketball schedule? Maybe this was nothing more than a coincidence.

She did her best to keep her expression neutral as Joey relived every moment of winning the basketball game.

"Did you see my last basket? The coach said it was amazing and that without my score we might not have won the game. Isn't that awesome, Mom?" he asked for the third time. "I can't wait until our next tournament. Coach said I can be in the starting lineup!"

"The game was awesome," she agreed, looking once again in her rearview mirror. Was the truck gaining on them? Darkness came early in December so it was hard to gauge the distance. She tightened her grip on the steering wheel and pressed down on the accelerator. For the first time she bemoaned the fact she'd traded in her high-powered sports car for a four-cylinder eco-friendly hybrid last year. The hybrid's engine chugged as she fought to increase her speed.

The truck edged closer, and she glanced helplessly around at the winding country road she'd taken to avoid the traffic on the interstate. Was the driver of the truck behind her the same person who'd sent her the threatening letters? Was he working for someone linked to the Mafia?

Swallowing hard, she drew her cell phone out of the front pocket of her sweatshirt and pushed the preprogrammed number for Nick Butler. He'd told her to call day or night and, thankfully, seven-thirty in the evening wasn't too late. She held her breath until he answered.

"Butler."

"It's Rachel. We're being followed by a black truck license plate number TYG-555. We're on Handover Road, just past Highway 12."

"Mom? What's going on?" Joey swiveled in his seat, finally realizing that something was wrong.

"Hang tight, I'm not far away. I'll be right there," Nick said in a calm, reassuring tone.

"Hurry," she urged, before sliding the phone back into her pocket and returning both hands to the wheel. She increased her speed more, wondering why Nick would be so close, when suddenly, the truck rammed into her from behind, causing the steering wheel to jerk in her hands as the car swerved dangerously. She and Joey were wearing their seat belts, but she wasn't sure the restraint would be enough to prevent them from being harmed. "Hang on, Joey!" she shouted as she fought to stay in control.

"Mom!" Joey screamed as the truck rammed into them again, and this time, she couldn't prevent the car from slamming into the guardrail with a sickening lurch. She tried to ride against the rail, but the car spun out of control, doing a complete three-sixty before hitting the side rail again, thankfully on the driver's side.

The impact caused the airbags to explode in their faces. Pain radiated through her face and chest. "Joey!" she shrieked, frantic to know her son was all right.

The car came to an abrupt halt, but the driver's side door was bent inward to the point of pinning her left foot. She batted away the air bags as she frantically reached over for her son. "Joey? Are you all right?"

"Yeah," he said, between hiccuping sobs. "I think so."

Coughing as air bag dust filled her lungs, she tried

again to get her foot out from the twisted hunk of metal. When that didn't work, she reached over to help Joey get out of his seat belt. "I need you to get out of the car, Joey. Run away and get help. Find Detective Butler. Do you understand me? You need to get away from here and find Detective Nick Butler."

"Not without you," he cried.

"I'll be right behind you," she said, even though she wasn't sure she'd be able to wrench herself free. "Now go. *Hurry!*"

Somehow, Joey managed to crawl out of the passenger-side window, which was completely busted open. She pulled, gritting her teeth against the pain as she tried to yank out her pinned foot.

Through the open window she saw Joey stagger a bit before he managed to pick up his pace enough to run. She heard the distant wailing of a police siren and hoped that was Nick, as she shifted in her seat again, determined to find a way to get free.

But then she saw a large man dressed completely in dark clothing, recognizing him as the driver of the big black truck that had caused her to crash. Through the glow of her headlights, she saw him take off running after her son. "No! Joey!" she screamed, ripping her foot out of her shoe, finally gaining freedom. *"No!"*

Too late. The tall stranger easily scooped up her son and dropped a black hood over Joey's head before taking off with him thrown over his shoulder like a sack of potatoes. Joey struggled against him, but the guy never hesitated, ignoring her son's kicks and punches.

"No!" she wailed, scrambling to get out of the crushed car. She threw herself across to the passenger seat and wiggled her way through the broken window. "Stop! Joey!"

But the moment she fell from the window onto the paved road, the big black truck engine rumbled to life and pulled away, tires screeching, with her son trapped inside.

TWO

Nick slammed his foot down hard on the accelerator, racing to Rachel's location, his heart pounding in his chest. Earlier that day, he hadn't been entirely convinced her stalker was really someone from the Mafia. But the threats had been enough that he couldn't bear to leave her totally on her own, so he'd followed Rachel to her son's basketball game without telling her he was nearby.

Now he realized his instincts had been right on. The panic in her tone gripped him by the throat and he couldn't help feeling that this was his fault for not doing more to keep her safe. He saw Rachel and Joey leaving the school after the game, but at that moment he'd taken a call from his boss, questioning why he'd taken on Rachel's stalker case. He'd explained about the possible mob connection, which had eased his captain's concern. But in the time it had taken him to placate his boss, Rachel and Joey had disappeared from sight.

His fault for not telling her he was there. And if something bad happened to Rachel and Joey, he'd never forgive himself. As he drove, he silently prayed for their well-being.

Please, Lord, keep Rachel and Joey safe in Your care. Amen.

The closer he got to the location she'd given him, the more his gut tightened with fear and worry. And when he saw her mangled car wedged against the guardrail, his stomach dropped. He was surprised to see there weren't any police cars or ambulances at the scene. As he pulled over, Rachel was there, limping and crying, making her way down the road. He bolted from his car and ran toward her. "Rachel, what is it? What's wrong?"

"He took Joey!" She grabbed his arm in a tight grip. "You have to do something! Right now!"

"Which way did they go?"

"N-north."

"All right, let's go." He took her arm since she was shaking so badly he was afraid she wouldn't be able to stay upright. She managed to hang on long enough to climb into his car. He slid quickly into the driver's seat.

As he drove he reached for the radio. "I have to call my boss, tell him to send a chopper. The truck will be easier to find from the air at night."

"Wait! I have a text message."

He froze, watching as she pulled her cell phone from the pocket of her pink hoodie sweatshirt.

"Oh, no," she whispered.

"What is it?"

"Don't call the police or I'll kill him." She lifted her tortured gaze to his. "I knew it! I knew the mob was after me. And now they've kidnapped Joey!"

Every instinct he possessed told him to radio for backup, but Rachel had grabbed his arm again, squeezing so tight he winced as her nails dug painfully into his skin. "We have to find him. We have to get to Joey!" she sobbed.

"Rachel, I know you're scared, but let's calm down and

think this through. We need to get the helicopters to go after that black truck."

"If that guy sees the police he'll kill Joey. You don't know how ruthless the Mafia can be. Please don't do anything that will hurt my son. *Please!*" Her green eyes implored him to listen.

He pressed harder on the accelerator, going well above the speed limit. He wished a cop would try to pull him over, because then they'd have their badly needed backup.

"This is all my fault. They have Joey and it's all my fault," Rachel moaned.

He glanced over at her, wishing there was something he could say to make her feel better. But he knew only too well what it was like to lose a child.

"There!" Rachel's excited shout drew him out of his depressing thoughts. "That's the black truck that hit me."

He couldn't believe they'd found the black truck here, on the side of the road. But as they came closer, it was clear that the vehicle had been abandoned. Was it possibly a different truck? No, the damage to the front bumper convinced him they had the right vehicle. The passenger-side door was left hanging wide open, as if someone had grabbed Joey and taken off running without bothering to shut the door behind him.

He scanned the area, but there wasn't much he could see in the darkness outside the glow from his headlights. He could tell that beyond the open cornfield was a subdivision full of houses, many of them twinkling with various holiday lights. The kidnapper could be anywhere. Either on foot or—if he wasn't working alone—in another vehicle.

"Where are they? Where's Joey?" Rachel barely waited for him to stop the car before she was out and racing over to see for herself.

He followed hot on her heels, ready to prevent her from disturbing any evidence. But he needn't have worried.

She simply stood there, staring inside the empty truck, her eyes welling with tears. "They're gone," she whispered.

He curled his fingers into helpless fists, knowing there wasn't any way to put a positive spin on this latest turn of events.

Joey was gone and Nick didn't have a clue as to where he might be.

Rachel shivered, ice creeping slowly through her bloodstream like a glacier. She'd been so certain they'd find the black truck. Find Joey.

But her son was still missing.

"Come on, Rachel. I have to call my boss," Nick urged, putting a hand beneath her elbow to nudge her away from the truck.

She didn't move, couldn't seem to tear her gaze from the empty truck. Joey had been in there, with a hood over his face. She couldn't bear to think of how frightened her son must be. "Hang in there, Joey," she whispered, as if he could hear her. "I'm coming to get you."

"Rachel, there's nothing more we can do here. Not until we get a forensic team to go through the truck to pick up trace evidence."

"No cops," she said weakly, even though she knew it was too late. Nick was a cop and she'd called him right before the crash. And obviously they needed all the help they could get to find Joey. Her frozen brain cells finally put a few pieces of the puzzle together. "How did you get to me so quickly?" she asked with a frown.

He shrugged and ducked his head before he abruptly turned away, heading back to his vehicle. She forced her legs to follow him, wincing as she stepped on a stone with her foot that didn't have a shoe.

"Wait," she said, stopping him once again as he reached for the radio. "Can you call this incident in as a hit-and-run? Without mentioning Joey?"

"Rachel, you know that's not smart," he said with a heavy sigh. "I get that they have you running scared, but the more people searching for your son, the better."

Logically, she could agree, but there was nothing logical about her feelings regarding the mob. And she was convinced that her husband's uncle, Frankie Caruso, was the mastermind behind Joey's kidnapping. "You don't understand," she said brokenly, wishing she could convince him. "If they get any sense that the police are involved there's nothing to stop them from killing him."

"Why would they kidnap your son in the first place?" he asked. "You have to admit, kidnapping is a huge leap from stalking."

She drew her arms across her jacket, trying to maintain some warmth in the cold December night. Her left ankle throbbed, but she shoved the pain aside. No matter how much she hurt, she wouldn't allow anything to stop her from finding her son. "Maybe the Mafia is looking for money from my company? Money that will help them rebuild their organization?"

"It's possible, since the Mafia has taken several big hits lately," Nick mused. "And you think they targeted you because of your marriage to Anthony?"

"Yes. Don't you see? It all fits! My father's money helped me escape Anthony all those years ago, so now they want me to pay them back. That's basically what those threatening notes said, right?"

Grimacing, Nick nodded slowly. "I guess in a twisted way, that makes sense."

She was dizzy with relief, knowing she'd finally managed to convince him of the Mafia link. "The mob fights dirty and plays for keeps," she murmured. "If you call in reinforcements, the dirty cops might find out and let Joey's captors know. I just can't take that chance."

"Not all cops are dirty, Rachel," Nick said, a hard edge to his tone.

She sensed she was losing the battle. "During my brief marriage to Anthony, I knew of several Chicago cops who were on his payroll. None of them would lift a finger to help me. Can you honestly say that there isn't the possibility of dirty cops still on the force?"

He scowled as he twisted the key in the ignition. "No, I can't tell you that as much as I wish I could. I hate knowing that some of the very men and women who are supposed to put criminals away actually join forces with them, instead. Kidnapping is a federal offense, so we could call in the FBI."

Fear tightened her chest to the point she felt she couldn't breathe. "Are you sure there isn't any possibility of someone linked to the Mafia working inside the FBI, too?"

Nick let the car idle as he scrubbed his hands over his face. "No, I can't tell you that, either. Because there was a dirty FBI agent involved in a case I worked on last summer. We arrested him, but I always wondered if there weren't others, too. Others that we missed."

The thought of losing her son was making bile rise to her throat. "Please, Nick. All I'm asking for is a little time. Please keep Joey's involvement out of this for now."

He turned his head and stared at her for a long moment. "I'm going to at least let my boss know what's going on. I know he's not dirty and we need someone to trust." She wanted to protest but knew that he had a job to do. Nodding stiffly, she dropped her hand from his arm so that he could call in a crime team to investigate the crash scene and the abandoned truck.

She didn't relax a single muscle until he disconnected the call, without once mentioning Joey. Unfortunately, her relief was short-lived when Nick punched in another number.

"Hey, I think we have another link to the Mafia angle," he said into the phone.

She strained to hear the other side of the conversation, which she assumed was with Nick's boss. "Yeah? Like what?"

Her heart squeezed when Nick briefly explained what had transpired. "I'd like to keep this quiet for now, while we wait for some more evidence. If the Mafia is behind this, there isn't much to stop them from doing something drastic if they sense we're onto them."

"I'm not sure I like that plan, Butler." She could hear Nick's boss's weary tone. "The feds won't be happy if we don't follow protocol."

"Yeah, but you and I both know that there have been far too many dirty cops, both locally and at the federal level. Just give me a little time to see what we can shake out, okay?"

"All right. But keep me posted."

"Will do." Nick hung up the phone and then put the car in gear.

"Thank you, Nick," she murmured softly.

"Don't thank me," he said in a harsh tone. "We don't have Joey back yet. And you need to know this may not turn out the way you want it to."

"We'll get him back." She wasn't even going to consider the possibility of failure.

He let out an exasperated sigh. "I hope so, but you have to understand that we don't have a lot of time. If we don't hear from the kidnappers soon, I won't give you a choice. We will call in the FBI."

She wanted to argue, feeling deep down that calling in the FBI would be the worst thing they could do. After all, she knew from personal experience how the Mafia worked. The members of the mob were cruel and ruthless and wouldn't hesitate to kill her son just to prove their point.

The threatening notes she'd received were right. She had screamed in agony when they'd kidnapped her son. And if they demanded a ransom, she would repay her debts in order to get him back.

Panic bubbled in her throat and she had to swallow the urge to start screaming all over again. She needed to stay calm, to think this through logically, if she was going to have any chance in finding Joey.

After several long deep breaths, she felt somewhat calm. "You never did mention how you reached me so quickly," she said, glancing over at Nick.

There was a long silence before he admitted, "I followed you and Joey. I guess I was hoping to catch the guy in the act of leaving another note for you."

He'd been sitting in the parking lot of the elementary school? She tried to grapple with that revelation. "I didn't see you," she said. "And believe me, I was on alert, searching for signs of Frankie or one of his thugs."

Nick shifted in his seat. "I stayed in my car, a little ways down the road, just close enough to watch your vehicle."

She wasn't sure that news was reassuring. If she hadn't seen Nick, maybe she'd missed the driver of the black truck, too? She couldn't bear the thought that she may have led the kidnapper straight to her son's location.

More deep breaths helped rein in her fear. She tried to

find comfort in the fact that Nick had cared enough to try to protect her, but the image of her son being kidnapped by the driver of the truck was seared in her mind.

Helplessly, she gazed down at her phone, looking at the text message again. Don't call the police or I'll kill him.

Why hadn't they already demanded money? That had to be the reason they'd kidnapped Joey. Nothing else made sense.

"We should probably stay in a hotel tonight," Nick said, breaking into her grim thoughts. "Especially because you received those threats at both your office and your home."

She pressed her fingertips against her aching temples, trying to think. "I guess a motel would be okay."

"It's our best option. For now."

She understood the warning implication in his tone. This was a temporary plan at best. She stared down at her cell phone for another long moment, willing the kidnapper to contact her again. The sooner they told her how much money they wanted, the sooner she could get her son back, safe and sound.

"Tell me what you know about Frankie Caruso," Nick said quietly.

Her stomach twisted into painful knots. "I'm afraid I don't know much. I only met him for the first time at our engagement party and then again at our wedding. I knew he'd raised Anthony after his parents died, but I didn't know about their link to the Mafia. Not until after we were married."

Nick glanced at her, and she wondered if he thought she was an idiot for not figuring out what was going on sooner. She'd often asked herself the same thing. She didn't like to think about how naive she was back then. She graduated college early and by twenty-five had worked her way up in her father's company to vice president. Hours of studying meant she hadn't dated much. Anthony had swept her off her feet with his dashing good looks and his charm.

It was only after they were married for a few months that she caught a glimpse of his dark side. But by then she'd discovered she was pregnant and tried to make the marriage work.

Until she was on the receiving end of his violent temper.

"Has Frankie been living here in Chicago?" Nick pressed.

"Early on, he did, but after Anthony won his second term as state senator, Frankie moved down to Phoenix. Anthony told me that his uncle was tired of the brutal Chicago winters."

"But you think Frankie's back in the area?"

She lifted her shoulders in a helpless shrug. "Honestly, I haven't kept track of Anthony's uncle in the years since our divorce. I was lucky to get away from Anthony early in our marriage, shortly after Joey's first birthday." Two years of marriage that had seemed like a lifetime. "I suspect that since Anthony is dead, Frankie might have come back to take his place within the Mafia."

"Rachel, there isn't much of the Mafia left for him to return to," he said. "I happen to know that Bernardo Salvatore and his right-hand man, Russo, are both dead."

The news surprised her. "Really? How?"

He pressed his lips into a grim line. "I can't go into details other than to tell you that I was there when they were killed. You have to consider there might be someone else besides Frankie Caruso after you."

"I'm telling you there's no one else I can think of," she said, wishing he would believe her. "Besides, if Salvatore and this Russo guy are dead, then it makes even more sense to me that Frankie came back to Chicago.

Clearly he wants to pick up the crime syndicate where Salvatore left off."

"Maybe. I'll try running a search on him," Nick murmured. "It's possible we'll get lucky."

She didn't bother to tell Nick that she didn't feel lucky. The thought of her son being held by the Mafia, alone and afraid, made fear clog her throat to the point she could barely breathe. Outside the passenger-side window, she stared at the holiday decorations lighting up people's houses. Would Joey be back in time for Christmas? She couldn't even imagine the possibility that he wouldn't be.

Nick pulled up to a low-budget motel and secured two connecting rooms. She reluctantly took her room key from his hand, knowing she couldn't relax, couldn't rest.

Not until she found her son.

"Rachel?" She glanced up when she heard Nick call her name from the open doorway between their rooms.

"What is it?" she asked, rising to her feet and crossing over to meet him in the doorway.

"Are you hungry?"

She grimaced and shook her head. "No." The mere thought of food made her nauseous. "You mentioned doing a search on Frankie Caruso. Do you have a laptop with you?"

"Yeah, I have my laptop," Nick replied. "So far, I haven't found much."

Frankie Caruso was too smart to leave an obvious trail. She kept her phone gripped in her hand, unable to bear the thought of losing the small link that she had with Joey's kidnapper. She hated to think of what her son might be suffering through right now. Why hadn't they contacted her again? What were they waiting for? "We have to keep searching. We have to find something!"

"Rachel, I know you're upset, but there isn't much more I can do. If we don't hear something soon, we'll have no choice but to pull in the FBI."

"No. We can't." The very thought of bringing in the authorities nearly made her double over in pain. "Your boss promised us some time, right? I'm sure the kidnappers will contact me soon."

"All right." There was a hint of disappointment in his gaze. She told herself she didn't care what Nick thought of her. He couldn't possibly imagine what she was going through. Or what she'd already suffered at the hands of the Mafia. She'd lived with Anthony for two long terrible years and had learned early on that confronting the Mafia directly only made them angry.

She didn't want the man who'd kidnapped Joey to take his anger out on her son.

"I'm going to get something to eat," Nick said over his shoulder. "Stay here and don't let anyone in except for me."

"Can I use your laptop while you're gone?" she asked.

He shrugged. "Sure, why not?"

She waited for him in the doorway, gratefully taking the computer from his hands. "Thank you."

"I'll be back soon," he said huskily, and he closed the connecting door on his side.

She opened the computer and tried to think of what little she remembered from those early days with Anthony—the places he went, the people he considered friends. She'd purposefully pushed all those bad memories out of her mind after she escaped, so dredging them up again wasn't easy.

Typing Frank Caruso's name into the search engine didn't bring up many hits. She tried using Luigi Gagliano's name too, as he was a distant cousin to Anthony.

Still nothing. And as she stared blankly at the computer, a terrible thought occurred to her.

Here she was, waiting for Joey's kidnappers to call with some sort of ransom demand, but what if she was on the wrong track? What if Frankie didn't want her money, but simply wanted her son?

Frankie had raised Anthony, bringing him into the world of crime at a young age. Was it possible he wanted to use Joey as a surrogate for Anthony?

Was it possible that Frankie was, right now, driving far away with her son?

Rachel's heart rate soared as she surged to her feet. Nick had been right! They should have called the police and the FBI right away! If Frankie had kidnapped Joey for personal reasons then he already had a head start on them.

She grabbed her phone, intending to call Nick, but then forced herself to stop and think. Why would Frankie send her threatening letters, saying she would repay her debts, if he didn't want money?

Pacing the length of the small motel room helped calm her ragged nerves. Her ankle throbbed, but she ignored it. She'd never had a panic attack like this before, not even in the dark days after Anthony had beaten her. She had to stop overreacting to every thought. Every remote possibility.

Somehow she had to be smarter than Frankie Caruso or Luigi Gagliano.

She sat down at the small desk and clicked on the mouse to reactivate Nick's computer. There was one angle she hadn't considered, and that was Frankie's ex-wife, Margie Caruso. Frankie and Margie had divorced the year Rachel was pregnant with Joey, but, surprisingly, they'd stayed on friendly terms. She'd often wondered if Margie had also been involved in illegal activities; otherwise, why wouldn't Frankie have tried to silence his ex-wife? After all, Anthony had often threatened to kill Rachel if she ratted him out.

Anthony's threats hadn't been empty ones, either.

And if Margie was part of the Mafia, it wasn't a stretch to think that she could be in cahoots with Frankie on this kidnapping scheme.

A quick search revealed that Margie was still living in the Chicago area. She wrote down the address, determined to convince Nick that they needed to pay the woman a surprise visit.

THREE

Nick couldn't stop thinking about Rachel and Joey as he ran a few errands. He understood what Rachel was going through—he'd been inconsolable after his wife and daughter went missing, too. He knew he shouldn't let his emotions get in the way of doing what was right, but seeing the pain etched on Rachel's face was impossible to ignore.

After picking up some new clothes he'd put a call in to his FBI buddy, Logan Quail, only to find out his friend was out of the country on his honeymoon. No wonder Logan hadn't returned his calls. The timing was unfortunate, since Logan's expertise would have been perfect for Rachel's situation.

But he'd just have to use another way to help Rachel find her son.

As he was picking up some fast food, his phone rang and he was surprised to discover that the caller was his boss, Ryan Walsh. "Hi, Captain."

"Butler. We have some news from the crash scene you called in earlier."

"You do?" He juggled the phone as he handed over cash and accepted the bag of food from the bored teen at the window. "What do you have?"

"We got a hit on one of the fingerprints. Perp's name is Ricky Morales and he's got a rap sheet, largely for drug busts, but, most recently, he was arrested for armed robbery. He just got out on bail about six months ago."

Nick pulled away from the drive-through window and parked in the first open slot he saw. "Do you think Morales has found a home working as a thug for the Mafia?"

His boss grunted. "Don't see why not. It's a lead worth following since the truck is registered in his name, too. Explains why he dumped his ride as soon as he did. I'll send his last-known address to you in an email. Where are you right now?"

"Getting something to eat." Nick didn't want to say too much. "We also have a possible suspect in Frankie Caruso, who happens to be Anthony Caruso's uncle. Ms. Simon is convinced that Frankie is back to take over the Mafia."

"What do you think?" Walsh asked.

"I think she could be right. You might want to see what you can find out about Caruso's activities. In the meantime, we'll start looking for leads related to Ricky Morales."

"Sounds like a plan." He could hear his boss scribbling notes. "Good work so far, Butler. Keep in touch."

"I will." Nick disconnected from the call and stared at his phone for a moment. He debated searching for Morales right now, but then decided he needed to get back to the motel. At least he had some positive news to give Rachel.

The drive didn't take long. He grabbed the clothes and the bag of food, his mouth watering at the aroma of burgers and fries, and swiped his key card. The moment he closed the motel door behind him, he heard Rachel knocking on the connecting door.

"Coming," he called as he reached for the door. He

smiled at her. "Don't argue, but I brought food for the both of us."

"There's no time to eat," Rachel said in a rush. "Look what I've discovered." She gestured to the computer screen. "Margie Caruso, Frankie's ex-wife still lives outside of Chicago. We have to get over there right away."

Her excitement was palpable. "Good news, but I have something to follow up on, too." He pushed the laptop out of the way so he could haul the food out of the bag. "I'll search while we eat."

Rachel frowned, but he noticed she was staring at the burgers and fries as if her appetite may have returned. He bowed his head and gave a quick prayer of thanks. Rachel didn't say anything, respecting his silent prayer, until he finished and dug into his food. "What are you following up on?" she asked.

"Sit down and eat," he suggested.

She grimaced, but came over to sit beside him. As if she couldn't help herself, she popped a French fry into her mouth. He waited until she surrendered to her inevitable hunger by unwrapping the second sandwich and taking a bite before telling her what his boss had uncovered.

"You think this Ricky Morales is the guy who kidnapped Joey?" she asked, her green eyes filled with hope. "I mean, that seems to be the most logical conclusion. And we should be able to find him, right?"

He nodded, even though he knew tracking Morales down wouldn't be quite that easy. As he ate, he pulled up his email and jotted down the information his boss had sent. "Here's his last-known address. It's on the opposite side of town from Margie Caruso's place."

"It's only eight-thirty…there's plenty of time yet to head over to see what we can find. I need to keep busy, searching for Joey We have to find him as soon as possible!"

"We'll check both addresses out tonight," he assured her.

"Thank you," she murmured.

He shook his head, not wanting her gratitude. He was beginning to identify with Rachel on a personal level. Her fear tugged at his heart. He knew, only too well, what she was going through. Those hours his wife and daughter were missing had been the longest, darkest hours of his life. And when the news came in that they were both found dead in their mangled SUV at the bottom of a ravine, his grief had been overwhelming. Without his faith, he never would have survived the dark days following their deaths.

Grimly, he hoped and prayed that Rachel's outcome would be different. *Please, Lord, keep Joey safe in Your care and guide us in finding him. Amen.*

Rachel pushed away her half-eaten sandwich and the remaining cold French fries, her patience wearing thin. She couldn't bear the thought of sitting here another minute. If she didn't take some sort of action to help find her son, she'd go stark, raving mad.

She tapped her fingers impatiently on the table, as Nick finished his meal. "I bought a dark sweatshirt for you, since that pink one is too easily seen at night, and a new pair of athletic shoes," he said between bites. "Also hats and gloves. Why don't you change while I finish up?"

"Okay, thanks," she said, reaching down for the bag of clothes. The shoes were a welcome sight, and while she loved her pink sweatshirt, she realized Nick was right about how it stood out. The black sweatshirt beneath her jacket would blend far better with the night.

She disappeared into the bathroom and quickly

changed. Her left ankle was swollen, but she managed to get that shoe on by loosening the laces. The pain in her foot was nothing compared to the gaping hole in her heart.

When she emerged from the bathroom, she was grateful to see that Nick had finished his meal, disposing of all the garbage in the trash can by the door. He'd pulled on the matching black sweatshirt, too, before zipping up his jacket. He shut down the computer and then turned to her. "Ready?" he asked, rising to his feet.

"Yes." She was more than ready. She tucked her room key into her back pocket and followed Nick out to the car. Once she was buckled in, he set his phone in the cradle where he could easily read the GPS directions.

"Where are we going first?" she asked.

"Morales lives closer," he said, glancing over his shoulder as he backed out of the driveway. "We'll go there, first."

She didn't argue with his logic. Granted, it wasn't likely that Morales would abandon his truck and take Joey to his home address listed on the registration, but, then again, criminals weren't always known for being smart.

The minutes ticked by with agonizing slowness as Nick drove through the night. She tensed when she noticed they were heading straight into a seedy part of town. Her stomach roiled at the thought of Joey being kept in a place where he was likely to be assaulted, or worse even, if he managed to escape.

"There it is," Nick murmured. "Second apartment building on the right."

"Do we know which apartment might be his?" she asked, leaning forward to see better. The dilapidated building sure wasn't comforting. "Do you really think he would have brought a kidnapping victim here to his place?"

"Doubtful, especially if he's working for someone else," Nick said. "I'm going to get out here to see if I can find out if he's still living here. Slide into the driver's seat and head around the block. This won't take long."

"All right." As soon as Nick pulled over and climbed from the vehicle, she slipped over the console and adjusted the seat so she could drive. "Be careful," she added before he shut the door.

He nodded and then pulled his sweatshirt hood over his head and hunched his shoulders as he loped across the street to the apartment building. As much as she wanted to watch, she forced herself to put the car in gear. At the end of the block was a stop sign and she turned right. There was a small group of tough-looking kids smoking cigarettes as they gathered at the street corner, beneath a streetlight where a small Christmas wreath was hanging. As she watched them she saw the gleam of silver. A knife? Or a gun? Several of them hid their hands in their pockets as she went past, giving her the distinct impression they were hiding something. Drugs? Maybe. Swallowing hard, she made sure the doors were locked before she gripped the steering wheel tightly.

As she came around the last corner to the street where Morales's apartment building was located, her heart sank when she saw the group of teens had moved down closer to the apartment building. Had they noticed Nick getting out of the car and going inside? What if they planned to rob him when he came out? This was a bad neighborhood, where crime ran rampant. She knew Nick carried his service weapon, but the odds were still stacked against him, especially since all six of them were likely armed, too.

She was fumbling with her cell phone, intending to call Nick to warn him, when he slipped out of the apartment building and headed down the steps. Her heart hammered in her chest as the group of kids stepped forward, cutting him off.

Nick kept his hand in the pocket of his jacket and she assumed he had his gun ready. He sidestepped the kids, but they crowded closer and once again, she caught sight of a flash of silver.

Rachel unlocked the car and leaned on the horn. The group of kids swung around in surprise, and in that split second, Nick ran around them and jumped into the car. "Go!" he shouted as he slammed the door shut.

She stomped on the accelerator and the car leaped forward. In her rearview mirror she saw the group of kids begin running after them. Did they still intend to rob them? Or worse? As she approached the stop sign up ahead, she glanced frantically both ways before ignoring the sign and going straight through the intersection without stopping.

"Take it easy," Nick said, putting a hand on her arm as she took another turn a little too fast. "They flashed a few knives and demanded money, but we're safe now."

She couldn't speak, could barely calm her racing heart enough to take a deep breath. Her entire body was shaking in the aftermath of their close call.

"Pull over up ahead," Nick instructed.

She knew he wanted to drive and couldn't blame him. She did as he requested, trying to hold herself together. She dragged herself out of the driver's seat as Nick came around to meet her. He lightly clasped her shoulders, peering down at her. From the streetlight behind her, she could see the concern etched on his handsome face.

"Are you all right?" he asked.

She tried to speak, but her throat felt frozen. It abruptly hit her how much she was depending on Nick to help find her son. If anything had happened to him, she'd be lost.

As much as she longed to lean against his strength, she forced herself to step back, putting distance between them. "I'm fine, but I was afraid they were going to hurt you," she confessed softly.

"Me, too, and I didn't really want to shoot any of them. Thanks to your quick thinking, I didn't have to. Now let's get going, okay?"

She nodded and went around to the passenger side of his car. "Did you find anything?" she asked, hoping the stop at the apartment building hadn't been in vain.

"Yeah. Morales still has a place there, apartment number 210 according to the mailbox. I spoke to the manager, but he claims he hasn't seen Ricky in weeks."

She tried not to be too discouraged by the lack of information. Truthfully, he'd found out more than she'd hoped. "I guess that means he's not likely keeping Joey there."

"I doubt it. There are too many nosey people around, like those thugs back there."

"I hardly think they'd be the types to turn Ricky in to the police," she said with a sigh.

Nick didn't say anything to the contrary, which only made her more depressed. "Are you still up for heading over to the ex-wife's place?" he asked, changing the subject.

"Yes." Granted she'd been terrified back there at the apartment building, but nothing was going to stop her from searching for Joey.

Nick glanced over at Rachel, marveling at the depth of her strength. Granted, she'd been scared to death back there at the apartment building, but that hadn't stopped her from doing what needed to be done.

He used his radio to request a search on the Morales apartment related to the hit-and-run case. The dispatcher agreed to send a couple of uniforms over. He didn't really think they'd find anything useful, especially since the manager had been all too willing to talk once he'd seen Nick's badge.

If Morales had been around, the manager would have told him so.

The trip to Margie Caruso's house took about twenty minutes. Her neighborhood was several steps up from where Morales lived. At least the houses were neat and clean for the most part, several decorated with Christmas lights.

The address indicated the house they were looking for was the third one on the right. Nick slowed down as he drove past the modest red brick home with the tan trim and black shutters. The entire place was dark, not a single light on inside the place that he could see.

"What do you think? Is anyone home?" Rachel asked.

"I don't know. It's about nine-fifteen, so I suppose Margie could already be asleep...." But it wasn't likely.

Maybe they were on the wrong track? Could be that Margie Caruso was living a normal peaceful life that had nothing to do with the Mafia or kidnapping Rachel's son.

"What's the plan?" she asked, keeping the house in sight as he drove by.

"Don't have one yet. It's not as if we can simply walk up and demand to search the place, even if someone answers the door."

"Why not? I could try talking to her," Rachel said impulsively. "We're both ex-Carusos and I can use that connection to feel her out."

He wasn't sure he liked the idea, but couldn't come up with anything better so he reluctantly nodded. "All right. I'll park on the street, in front of the neighbor's house.

If anything seems off, you need to get out of there right away."

"I will." She hesitated for a moment before reaching for the door handle. Extremely bright lights bloomed in his rearview mirror as a car headed straight for them.

"Wait!" Nick shouted, reaching out to grab her arm. She paused, half in and half out of the car, so he yanked her back inside at the same time gunfire echoed through the night.

FOUR

"Get down!" he yelled, stomping on the gas and peeling away from the curb. He kept a hold on Rachel while she managed to get her legs tucked inside the car. He let go long enough to take a sharp right-hand turn, which caused the half-open passenger-side door to slam shut.

"What's going on?" Rachel asked.

"Stay down," he barked. Glancing at the rearview mirror, he could see the vehicle was keeping pace behind them. He could tell by the high yet narrow set to the headlights that it was a Jeep.

He had to figure out a way to lose it and fast.

"Why is he shooting at us?" Rachel gasped, her eyes wide with fear.

He shook his head, unable to answer as he concentrated on losing the gunman. He took several more turns, dodging around various vehicles in his way. Thankfully, traffic was relatively light this far outside the city, or escaping the shooter would have been impossible.

When there was a gap in traffic, he jerked the steering wheel to the left, taking the car up and over the curb, making an illegal U-turn. It wasn't easy keeping his eyes on the road while watching the Jeep behind him. The other car didn't make the turn right away, which was reassuring.

He immediately took another right-hand turn, putting even more distance between them. When he found an on-ramp for the interstate, he took it and pushed the speed limit as hard as he dared until he found the next exit. On that road, he switched directions, heading left.

Fifteen minutes later, he was convinced he'd lost the Jeep. "Are you all right?" he asked, as Rachel eased upright and reached for her seat belt. "He didn't hit you, did he?"

"I don't think so," she said, patting her arms and legs as if she wasn't entirely sure. "Did you get the license plate number? Do you think that was Joey's kidnapper?"

"I didn't get the plate number because I was blinded by his high-beam lights." He tried to figure out what had just happened. The whole event was weird. "Don't you think it's odd that he took a shot at us, but didn't keep firing? And that he didn't target anything important?"

"What do you mean nothing important? He almost hit us!" Rachel protested.

"Not even close," he argued mildly. "We were practically sitting ducks and he didn't hit either of us, or any significant parts of the car, like the gas tank or wheels. It's almost as if he wanted to scare us more than kill us."

"So it must have been Joey's kidnapper!" Rachel's tone had a note of excitement. "He didn't want to kill us, because he still wants the money."

"Maybe," he agreed, although the scenario didn't quite feel right. This entire case wasn't like anything he'd experienced before. He knew crooks, had investigated them for years and they always had a reason for what they did.

Only this time, nothing made sense.

He took the next exit off the freeway, slowing his speed to the posted limit.

"We have to go back there," Rachel said urgently, interrupting his train of thought. "To see if we can find Joey. We must have been close if they were so desperate to scare us away."

"Rachel, calm down for a minute and think this through. How did they find us outside of Margie Caruso's house in the first place? I made sure no one followed us when we left Morales's apartment building."

"I don't know, maybe it was all just a big coincidence? Morales could be working for Margie Caruso, and maybe he just pulled up as we got there."

"I don't think so." Nick hated to burst her bubble, but she wasn't thinking rationally. He pulled off onto the side of the road and turned in his seat to face her. "Even if he saw us there, how could he know we were the ones in the car?"

"Maybe he recognized your car from the crash site?"

"I came in from the south and you said he went north," he reminded her gently. "Rachel, they have your cell phone number. They sent you a text, threatening to kill Joey if you called the police. Don't you see? The only thing that makes sense is that they've tracked us through the GPS in your cell phone."

Rachel swallowed hard as she stared down at her cell phone. Was Nick right? Had they really tracked them through her phone? She wasn't a techno-geek so she had no clue how to even do something like that.

But she knew the possibility existed.

And if Nick's hunch was correct, then Joey's kidnapper already knew she wasn't alone.

Fear swelled in her throat, choking her as tiny red dots swam before her eyes.

"Breathe," Nick commanded, giving her shoulder a shake.

She didn't even realize she was holding her breath. She took a shaky gasp of air and lifted her tortured gaze to his. "They're always going to know where we are, aren't they? We're never going to be able to escape."

"Not unless we ditch your phone," he said grimly.

She clenched the phone so hard she was surprised she didn't break it in half. "No. No way. This is the only connection I have to Joey. This is the number they're going to use in order to contact me for the ransom demand. I'm not giving it up, Nick. I'm not! *I can't!*"

He stared at her for a long moment before releasing a heavy sigh. "Okay, if you're not getting rid of it, then we need to figure out our next steps. Because the kidnappers are going to be able to find us, no matter what we do or where we go."

"What if we buy a new phone, but keep the same number?" she asked suddenly. "Wouldn't that work? I mean, the GPS is linked to the device, not to the actual phone number…right?"

Perking up, Nick flashed her a smile. "You're brilliant, Rachel. That's exactly right. Now we have options."

"Do you think the stores are still open?" she asked.

"There are plenty of twenty-four-hour superstores. Here, use my smartphone to find the nearest one…."

"Okay." She took the phone and used the search engine to find the closest superstore. "There's one about seven miles away," she told him.

"Perfect."

They arrived at the superstore and quickly made their way over to the electronics section. She stayed back as Nick purchased the phone, along with a car charger, explaining to the clerk how they wanted to keep the same number.

"We can do that," the clerk said. "But it can sometimes take up to twelve hours to get the number transferred over."

"Twelve hours?" she echoed in shock.

The clerk shrugged. "It might be quicker, but I can't say for sure when."

Nick's expression was grim but he purchased the new phone and car charger, paying for a full year so that there wasn't any way to trace the contract fee. He gave her the phone and she stared down at it.

Twelve hours. She had to hang on to her old phone and evade the kidnappers for the next twelve hours.

And they were no closer to finding Joey.

She wanted to scream in frustration but forced herself to take several deep breaths to fight off her rising panic instead. She had to believe the kidnappers would keep Joey alive in order to get the payout. They had to.

She followed Nick to the car. When he started the car and pulled out of the parking lot, back onto the road, she plugged the new phone into the charger and then glanced at him. "Where are we going?"

He shrugged. "I think it's better to stay in the car and keep moving for now. We'd only be sitting ducks in a motel."

She couldn't argue his logic. "Would you be willing to split up so one of us could go and check out Margie's house? I need to know for sure Joey's not in there."

Nick was silent for so long she thought he was ignoring her. "Rachel, you're not a cop...so no, I'm not willing to split up. Let's just worry about staying alive tonight, okay? Unless you're having second thoughts about going to the FBI?"

She shivered. "No, I'm not having second thoughts. I heard what you told your boss about dirty cops at the local and federal level. I can't risk losing my son, Nick. I just can't."

He sighed. "I know what I said, but I can't help wondering if God isn't trying to tell us something the way these obstacles keep getting thrown in our way."

She was a little uncomfortable by his reference to God, but just the thought of calling in the police made her sick. "Your boss is willing to give us some time, so why are you still pushing the authorities on me?" When he opened his mouth to protest, she held up her hand. "I trust you, Nick, and I don't have much choice but to trust your boss, too. But I can't take the chance of trusting the wrong person. It could end up costing my little boy his life."

Truthfully, it was hard enough to trust Nick. But the fact that he'd been so angry with her for not giving him details about Anthony's involvement with the Mafia a year ago had gone a long way in convincing her that he was one of the good guys.

However, that didn't mean she wanted to open the circle of trust to include anyone else. Not unless there was no other choice.

Nick pulled into a mall parking lot, and she wasn't surprised when he positioned the car in a way that they'd be able to escape in a hurry if need be. She shivered a little, burying her face in the collar of the dark sweatshirt beneath her jacket. Her jean-clad legs were cold, and she rubbed her hands on her thighs to try and warm up.

"I have a blanket in the trunk," Nick said gruffly, before sliding out of the driver's seat. He returned a few minutes later with a wool blanket. "Why don't you stretch out in the backseat?"

"I won't be able to sleep," she protested. "Besides, we should take turns keeping watch."

"I'll keep watch first while you try to get some rest." His tone indicated there was no point in arguing.

Resigned, she opened the passenger door, pausing for a moment as she realized there was a bullet hole near the bottom of the window. The reminder of being used for target practice made her shiver again. Clutching the blanket, she climbed into the backseat and huddled down, grateful for the added warmth from Nick's blanket. She vowed to give him the blanket when it was her turn to keep watch.

The backseat was hardly comfortable, but that wasn't the reason she couldn't sleep. Images of Joey kept flashing through her mind, haunting her to the point where she almost couldn't stand it another moment.

"Nick?" she said softly, breaking the silence. "You don't think the kidnappers will hurt Joey, do you?"

"Try not to torture yourself thinking the worst, Rachel."

"I'm not trying to torture myself, but every time I close my eyes I picture that man grabbing Joey and slinging him over his shoulder. Don't you see? I'm the one who told Joey to get out of the car and run. It's my fault he was kidnapped."

There was a long pause, then Nick said, "Rachel, it's not your fault. I'm sure he would have gotten Joey even if you hadn't told him to run."

"Stop trying to placate me," she said sharply.

There was another brief silence. "Look, Rachel, I don't know if you believe in God, but if you do, praying can help you get through this."

She remembered how Nick had prayed before eating their fast-food dinner. Maybe he believed but she wasn't sure she did. "My parents weren't very religious. When I was growing up the only time we went to church was at Christmas and Easter." She hadn't thought about church or God in a long time. "I'm not sure I believe there really is a God, or that He cares anything about me or Joey."

"There is." Nick's voice exuded confidence. "And He does care about you and Joey. If you keep an open mind and an open heart, you'll be rewarded."

"Rewarded?" She couldn't hide the sarcasm in her tone. "I hardly think having my son kidnapped is anything close to rewarding."

"You're twisting my words, Rachel," he said quietly. "I meant that God can help you through difficult times."

"There's nothing more difficult than having your child in danger." She fought the rising anger. Who was he to preach to her at a time like this? Her son was missing and he wanted her to pray?

"I do know a little about what you're going through, Rachel. Two years ago, I lost my wife and my daughter in a terrible car crash. I nearly went crazy during the hours they were missing, before they were found dead in the bottom of a ravine. And trust me, I wouldn't have made it through those dark days without God's strength and the power of prayer."

His blunt statement surprised her and caused her to feel ashamed. Why was she taking her anger out on Nick? None of this was his fault. Clearly, he knew what it was like to lose someone he loved. Losing his wife and a daughter had to have been horrible. But prayer? She wasn't sure she was buying that idea.

She couldn't remember the last time she'd prayed, if ever. And she wasn't sure that prayer alone would make her feel better about losing her son.

She wouldn't survive if Joey died. Everything inside her would die right along with him.

"I've been praying for Joey's safety," Nick went on in

a low voice. "And I want you to know, I'll keep on praying for Joey and for you."

Tears pricked her eyes and her throat swelled, making it hard to speak. Knowing that he would pray for her son brought a surprising level of comfort. And she suddenly realized that he was right. She did need to keep an open mind. Because if Nick's prayers could really help, she would gladly take them. She would take anything she could get if it meant keeping Joey safe.

She cleared her throat, trying to hide the evidence of her tears. "Thank you, Nick. And I'm sorry I snapped at you. I didn't know you lost your wife and daughter. I guess you really do know what I'm going through."

"For a long time I wanted to join them up in heaven," he admitted. "But God chose another path for me, so I've decided to dedicate my life to putting bad guys away and leading a Christian life, until God calls me home to be with my family."

She wasn't sure what to say in response to that, since truthfully, his plan sounded a bit lonely. Although who was she to argue about being alone? She wasn't interested in having a relationship again, either, especially not while she was raising her son. She was too afraid to trust her instincts about men after the way she'd messed up with Anthony.

Was Nick subtly warning her that he wasn't interested in being anything more than friends? If so, she was happy to oblige.

Right now, she didn't care about anything except getting her son back safe and sound.

As the minutes passed slowly, she stared out through the car window at the stars scattered across the night sky.

And suddenly, she found herself uttering a simple prayer to a God she wasn't even sure existed.

Please keep my son safe.

FIVE

Rachel must have dozed in spite of herself, because, when she opened her eyes, dawn was breaking over the horizon and she didn't recognize the area. She assumed Nick had driven somewhere else at some point in the middle of the night. It took a moment for her to realize the beeping noise that woke her up came from a phone. She scrambled around, searching for her phone as Nick twisted in the driver's seat to look at back at her.

"Another text message?" he asked.

She pushed the button on her old phone and her heart leaped into her throat at the message that bloomed on the screen.

Ten million dollars will buy your son's freedom. Details on the exchange to follow. Remember, no police or your son will pay the price.

She tore her gaze from the message and held up the phone to show Nick. "It's the ransom demand," she said in a choked voice. She wasn't sure if she should be relieved or worried that the message had come so early in the morning.

She stared at the phone, wanting desperately to believe

that some sort of contact from the kidnappers was better than nothing.

"Text them back that you need proof that Joey is still alive," Nick ordered, starting the car and driving out of the parking lot. "Tell them you want to talk to your son."

She hesitated, afraid that if she made the kidnappers mad they might hurt Joey.

"Rachel, you have to know Joey is alive, or there's no point in agreeing to the demand."

Although she hated to admit it, she knew he was right. She took a deep breath and texted back, No money until I speak to my son.

The moment she pressed Send, she wanted to call the message back. She stared at her old phone for several long moments, hoping the kidnapper would respond. With every minute that ticked by, raw fear rose in the back of her throat, suffocating her.

"What if they don't let me talk to him?" she asked, unable to hide the quiver in her voice. "What if they hurt him, instead?"

"You have to insist on it," Nick said, a hard edge of steel lining his tone. "Please trust me on this, Rachel."

"I do, it's just that I don't care about the money," she whispered in agony. "I just want them to give me Joey."

"I know that, and believe me, they know that, too. They're playing on your fear, Rachel. They're doing this to keep you off balance. You have to be strong. For Joey."

She nodded, but the vise grip around her heart wouldn't loosen. She wanted to talk to Joey. Desperately needed to hear his voice.

Please, God, please keep Joey safe.

Just when she was about to give up all hope, her old phone rang, from another blocked number. She pushed the button and lifted the device to her ear. "Hello? Joey?"

"Mommy? Are you there?"

Hearing her son's voice made her eyes well up with tears. "Yes, Joey, I'm here. Are you okay? They didn't hurt you, did they?"

"No, but I'm scared," Joey said, and she could tell he was crying, too.

"Ask him something that only he knows," Nick whispered from the front seat. Belatedly, she realized he'd pulled off to the side of the road. "To prove it's him and not some other kid playing the part."

She nodded, indicating she'd heard him. "Joey, sweetheart, listen to me. Everything's going to be okay. But I need you to tell me who your favorite basketball player is. Can you do that for me?"

"K-Kirk Hinrich."

Yes! The starting point guard for the Chicago Bulls was Joey's favorite player. "That's good, Joey. I love you. I'm going to get you out of there soon, okay?"

"That's enough." A mechanically distorted voice broke into her conversation with her son. "We will give you details about the exchange soon."

"Wait!" she shouted, but nothing but silence was on the other end. She stabbed the button on her phone to call the blocked number back, but all she heard was a weird click then nothing. It took every ounce of willpower she possessed not to scream in frustration. But nothing could stop her tears.

"Don't cry, Rachel," Nick said in a low, soothing voice. "We're better off now than we were a few minutes ago. At least we know Joey's alive and that they're going to set up the exchange."

Nick was right, but she couldn't seem to stem the flowing tears. Just hearing Joey's voice made her furious with the kidnappers all over again. Her son was alone and afraid. "We have to find him," she sobbed.

He reached over the back of the seat to gently squeeze her shoulder. "We will. Remember God is watching over him, too."

Despite how she'd already prayed twice for her son's safety, Nick's words were far from reassuring. Because suddenly she couldn't understand why, if there really was a God, He would put an innocent nine-year-old boy in this kind of danger.

"I don't believe that," she said abruptly, pulling away from his reassuring touch. She used the bottom of her sweatshirt to mop her face. "I don't trust a God who allows my son to be in danger. And I can't understand how you could believe that, either."

Nick stared at her for a long minute, his gaze shadowed by a deep sorrow, before he wordlessly turned away and began driving again.

She ducked her head, swiping away the moisture from her cheeks. She shouldn't feel guilty for hurting him, but she did. Yet, at the same time, she couldn't bring herself to apologize, either.

Right now, nothing mattered except Joey. That was how she'd lived her life since leaving Anthony. A woman on a mission to provide a normal life for her son, keeping him safe from harm.

This wasn't the time to allow herself to get distracted. By Nick or by the God he believed in.

Nick drove to the truck stop he'd passed earlier, so they could use the restrooms and get something to eat. He tried not to be hurt by Rachel's anger as he understood, better than most, what she was going through. He'd been angry with God, too, at first when he'd discovered his wife and child had died. Anger was a normal part of the grief process, but that didn't mean he was giving up on her.

He'd continue praying for both Joey and Rachel.

Besides, she needed to cling to the knowledge of her son being safe and sound. There was still hope that they could figure out a way to get him back.

Rachel didn't say anything when he pulled into the truck stop parking lot, bringing the car to a halt between a pair of twin semitrailers. He climbed out of the driver's seat and then glanced back at her. "I thought we'd clean up in the restrooms first. I'll meet you in the diner in about fifteen minutes or so, okay?"

She nodded and pushed her way out of the car to join him. Wordlessly, they walked inside together before splitting up.

His stomach growled and the scent of bacon and eggs caused him to hurry. He scrubbed his hands over his rough stubble, wishing he had a razor. When he finished up in the restroom, he slid into a booth next to the door and perused the menu while he waited for Rachel.

She joined him a few minutes later and he didn't waste any time in placing their orders. Once they were alone with their coffee, he leaned forward and said firmly, "We need to figure out what to do from here, Rachel. Ten million is a lot of money."

"I know." She stared at her coffee, her hands huddled around it for warmth, but she didn't drink any.

"I know you're the CEO and president of your company, but are you really going to be able to get that much together?"

Slowly, she shook her head. "The economy has been tough, and we've had a large class-action lawsuit that has eaten away a significant portion of our profits."

Lawsuit? How come she hadn't mentioned this earlier? "What was the lawsuit about?"

She grimaced before answering. "We put a new diabetes medication on the market about two years ago. In clinical trials it was superior in performance to the medication that almost two-thirds of the diabetes patients are currently taking." She hesitated for a moment. "But something went wrong, and several people suffered very bad side effects and two patients died. The FDA mandated that we pull the drug off the market, and the lawsuit was filed shortly thereafter."

He stared at her in shock, mentally kicking himself for not investigating this angle earlier. "Rachel, isn't it possible that Joey's disappearance could be linked to this lawsuit rather than the Mafia?"

She sighed and lifted her gaze to his. "I don't see how the lawsuit could be related. I authorized a large settlement for those patients and their families. They deserve to be compensated for our mistake. What reason would they have to come after me now?" She gripped the mug tighter in her hands. "Besides, does it really matter who took Joey? All we need to do is to figure out a way to get him back."

It did matter, but he didn't say anything as the waitress headed their way with two plates of food. She plopped them down on the table, and then glanced at the two of them. "Need anything else?"

He forced a smile. "No thanks, we're fine."

The waitress turned on her rubber-soled heel and strode away. He bowed his head and prayed. *Thank You, Lord, for this food we are about to eat, and please keep Joey safe in Your care. Guide us in our journey to find him and help Rachel open her heart and her mind to Your peace and Your glory. Amen.*

When he opened his eyes, he realized Rachel had her head down, waiting for him to finish before eating her breakfast. She didn't join him in prayer, but she didn't lash out against God again, either, which he chose to believe was a good sign.

He dug into his bacon and eggs, savoring every bite. When the knot of hunger in his stomach had eased, he glanced up at Rachel again, noting with satisfaction that she was doing a good job of demolishing her own meal. "Tell me more about this lawsuit."

She lifted one shoulder. "There's nothing to tell."

"How is it that you didn't find the side effects of the medication during the clinical trials?" He didn't know much about the pharmaceutical industry, but surely there would have been an indication of the dangerous side effects long before the medication was released to the public.

Rachel tapped her fork on the edge of her plate. "That's one of the things I've been working on with my research team. We don't know why the blood clots only showed up after the medication was approved. The FDA wants a full investigation, and we're actually in the middle of pulling everything together." She sighed, and then added, "At least we were. Until all this happened."

The timing couldn't be a coincidence. "Who benefits if your company goes out of business?"

"No one." She set her fork down and pushed her half-eaten plate away. "My company employs well over three thousand people, who would all be out of a job if something happened. I can't see how this could be connected to Joey in any way."

He found it impossible to ignore the sliver of unease. "Rachel, be honest with me. Is your company in danger of going under?"

"Not yet, but we can't afford to take another hit like

the one we took earlier this year. So far, we've managed to weather the storm."

Relieved by that news, he continued to finish his breakfast. "What about your competition? Wouldn't they benefit if you went belly-up?"

"I can't imagine any company going to these lengths to get rid of the competition. You're on the wrong track, Nick. Those threatening notes have the Mafia written all over them."

She could be right. "You better eat," he advised. "There's no telling when we'll get our next meal."

She picked up her fork. "As soon as we're finished here, I need to call Gerry Ashton, my vice president of Operations."

"Why?"

"Because he's my second in command and owns forty percent of the company stock. I'm fairly certain he'll be willing to buy my shares. And I know his wife has a significant amount of money."

His stomach clenched at hearing her plan. "Do you think something that drastic is really necessary?"

She shrugged and toyed with her food. "Yeah, I do. Besides, I'd give up my company in a heartbeat if it meant getting Joey back safe and sound."

As Nick finished up and paid their bill, he couldn't help wondering if this was exactly what the lawsuit victims had planned all along. Forcing Rachel to give up everything she owned in order to save her son.

Rachel glanced at the clock, wondering if she dared call Gerry this early on a Thursday morning. They were both generally early risers, but it was barely seven-fifteen. She couldn't deny the deep sense of urgency. What if the kidnappers called right away, wanting the exchange? What if she didn't have enough time to pull the money together?

Logically, she knew that they would give her some time—after all getting the money was the end goal. Wasn't it?

She wished Nick hadn't questioned her about the lawsuit, because now uncertainty gnawed away at her. But those messages *had* to be from Anthony's uncle Frank, or from someone else within the Mafia. Nothing else made sense. Once they were back in Nick's car, she scrolled through her old phone's list of contacts until she found Gerry's cell number. Just as she pushed the button to call him, another text message came through. Another message from the kidnappers?

No, it was the text message stating that her phone number had been successfully transferred to her new phone. "Finally," she muttered.

"What?" Nick asked.

After she filled him in, Rachel got busy activating the new device. She had to click on a link first and then wait another few minutes for the phone number to be registered before she could use her new phone. When that was finished, she typed in Gerry's number and waited anxiously for him to pick up.

There was no answer, so she left a message. "Gerry, it's Rachel. Call me as soon as you get this. It's urgent."

Nick filled up the gas tank at the truck stop and dumped her old phone in the garbage before he slid behind the wheel and drove back out toward the highway. "Where does Gerry live?"

"About fifteen miles west of our corporate offices," she answered.

Nick glanced her way. "Okay, we're a good hour away, so I'm going to head in that general direction."

She nodded, hoping Gerry would call her back soon.

Forty-five minutes passed before her new phone rang, and she pounced on it when she saw Gerry's number come across the screen. "Hello?"

"Hi, Rachel, what's going on? What's so urgent?"

She relaxed a bit, hearing the sound of his voice. "Gerry, I'm so glad you called me back. I need your help. Would you mind meeting with me right away?"

"Of course, but why? What's wrong?"

"I'd, uh, rather explain in person."

"Okay, well then why don't you come to my house? We'll have plenty of privacy as Nancy is out visiting her mother, helping her recover from her hip surgery."

Nancy was Gerry's wife and she vaguely remembered that he'd mentioned Nancy's mother needing surgery. "That sounds perfect," she said, feeling relieved to know that Nancy wouldn't be there. "I'll see you in about fifteen minutes or so."

Asking Gerry for money wouldn't be easy—he'd been like a father figure to her since her own father had passed away from a sudden heart attack. She didn't like the thought of selling off her company, but she didn't have a choice. She'd give up everything she owned if it meant getting her son back safe and sound.

"You're not going to see him alone," Nick said, breaking into her thoughts.

She glanced at him in surprise. "I wasn't planning to."

He scowled as he navigated the streets heading toward Gerry's house. "But you didn't mention that you'd be coming with someone," he muttered.

"I didn't want to put him on guard," she admitted. "I'm not sure how much I should tell him."

"As little as possible," Nick responded. "No sense in dragging him into this mess."

"You're right. It's bad enough that I'm asking him to bail me out by buying my shares of company stock. And we still have to find a way to convince the bank to bypass their normal requirements to give me the cash immediately."

"One step at a time," he advised.

Gerry's house was much grander than hers, but then again, she preferred the family-friendly neighborhood she'd chosen to raise Joey in. There was nothing better than watching the neighborhood kids get together to play a quick game of soccer or baseball in the park across the street.

She had to shove the poignant memories aside. She needed to believe Joey would play again in the park, as soon as they got him away from the kidnappers.

"This is it," Nick said, as he pulled up into the driveway. There was a large wreath on the door and she could see the twinkling lights of a Christmas tree through the window. "Are you ready?"

She nodded and slowly climbed out of the car. She rang the doorbell and braced herself as Gerry swung open the door. He looked surprised to see Nick standing beside her. "Hi, Rachel, come on in."

She stepped across the threshold and then turned to make introductions. But before she could speak, Nick thrust his hand out. "Gerry, my name is Nick and I'm a good friend of Rachel's. I'm so glad we finally have a chance to meet in person, after all I've heard about you."

Her mouth dropped open, and she quickly closed it again. Nick's message was clear—he did not want to be introduced as a detective.

Gerry accepted Nick's handshake. "Nice to meet you, too," he said, throwing a suspicious gaze at Rachel. "I have to say, Nick, you have the advantage here, because Rachel hasn't mentioned you to me at all."

The reproach in his tone was obvious and she swallowed hard, already hating the way she wasn't being completely up-front and honest with Gerry.

"Gerry, I'm sorry to bother you," Rachel said abruptly. "I'm in trouble. Financial trouble."

His eyebrows furrowed together as he gestured for them to come in and sit down in the living room. "What do you mean by financial trouble?"

She twisted her hands in her lap, unable to hide her nervousness. This was extremely important and she couldn't afford to have Gerry refuse her request. "I can't tell you, so please don't ask. I need a lot of money, and I'm hoping you'll be willing to buy my shares of stock in the company."

The stunned expression on Gerry's face would have been comical if the situation wasn't so grim. "Rachel, I'm happy to loan you whatever you need. There's no reason to sell your stock."

His offer was humbling, but she knew she couldn't take him up on it. Gerry was in his late forties and his two sons were currently enrolled in college. She couldn't take advantage of his generosity. "I insist on selling them to you. That way, if anything happens…" She couldn't bring herself to finish her thought. "It's just better this way, because I need ten million dollars."

"Are you kidding me?" Gerry leaped to his feet and began to pace. "Rachel, that just about covers all your stock! And how are you going to get the bank to give you that much money?"

"I'm hoping Edward Callahan, the bank manager, will bend a few rules for me," she said. "He knows the company is worth far more than that."

Gerry let out his breath in a huff and then turned to glare at Nick. "Can't you talk her out of this nonsense?" he demanded.

"I'm afraid not. Rachel is the one in charge here. I'm just helping her out as a good friend."

Gerry's gaze narrowed and he threw up his hands. "All right, fine. I'll help you. But, Rachel, please reconsider taking a simple loan. There's no reason to sell off your stock from your father's company."

His offer was generous, but she shook her head stubbornly. She'd never sleep at night with that heavy a debt hanging over her head. "I need you to buy the stock, Gerry. I want everything legal. Please don't fight me on this."

She couldn't explain that the likelihood of getting the money back was slim to none. And besides, if something happened to her during the exchange, she wanted the company to be in good hands. Gerry would be able to pick up where she'd left off without any trouble.

And even if she did survive, she knew full well that, after this was all said and done, she and Joey would have to start over, with a new job and maybe even a new house.

A price she was willing to pay if it meant getting her son back safe.

SIX

Nick watched the interchange between Gerald Ashton and Rachel with interest. There was no denying the gentleman, who he guessed was roughly ten years their senior, seemed to care about Rachel. There was a casual familiarity between them as they ironed out the details of obtaining the money. While they worked, he swept a curious gaze around the room.

Family photos featuring Gerald, his wife, Nancy, and their two grown sons were proudly displayed. The furnishings in the room, including the holiday decorations, were expensive and fancy—not to his taste at all but not awful, either. The place looked like something out of a fashion magazine, and he didn't doubt for a moment that a professional decorator had had a hand in the outcome.

He'd never been to Rachel's house and wondered if her style was similar to Gerry's. Not that he should care one way or the other. But somehow, he couldn't imagine Rachel raising Joey in a fancy, formal place like this.

Or maybe that was wishful thinking on his part.

He had to admit there was nothing to make him think Gerry was anything but what he seemed—a wealthy businessman who cared about his family and about Rachel. He told himself to relax and tuned back into the conversation.

"I'll call Edward," Gerry told Rachel, putting a reassuring arm around her shoulder. Nick had to grit his teeth to stop from going over to forcibly remove it, even though the gesture was clearly intended to be reassuring and friendly. "I'm sure we can come up with some way to get you the cash you need. But the earlier I call him, the better."

"We appreciate your help, Gerry," Nick said, determined to make his presence known. He was more than willing to play the role of Rachel's boyfriend, if necessary. "Rachel said such kind things about you, I'm glad to see she was right."

Gerry actually looked flustered by the compliment. He removed his arm from Rachel's shoulders and pulled out his phone. "Give me a few minutes to talk this through with Edward, okay? We'll have to sign the paperwork in front of a notary, too, and he'll have someone at the bank we can work with, I'm sure."

"Thanks, Gerry."

While the older man was making the call, Nick crossed over to kneel by Rachel's side. "Are you okay?" he asked. As far as he could tell, she was holding up pretty well, considering.

"I will be once we have the cash," she murmured in a low voice. "At least we're one step closer to getting Joey back."

"Agreed. Just hang in there a little longer, okay?"

She nodded again but was still twisting her fingers together. He gently put his hand over hers, stilling her motions. "We'll get through this, Rachel," he said reassuringly. He wanted to invite her to pray with him but, after her outburst in the car earlier, settled instead on praying silently for her and Joey.

When Gerry returned, Nick rose to his feet. Rachel

stood, too, and he stayed close by her side. Gerry's gaze was openly curious as it moved between the two of them, but he didn't comment. "Edward is going to do his best to pull the funds together. He's asked that you call him in two hours. We can meet him at the bank to finalize everything."

"Sounds good. Thanks again, Gerry." She set the drafted forms aside. "Bring these with you, okay? I'll see you in a little while."

Gerry hesitated before taking the documents she'd handed over. "I feel terrible about this, Rachel, and my offer still stands. If something changes, and you still have the money, I'd be more than happy to rip this agreement up as if it never happened."

"Thanks, Gerry." Rachel's smile was heartbreaking, and she reached up to kiss Gerry's cheek before turning away. Nick followed, as they made their way back outside.

In the car, he turned toward her, half expecting tears, but her eyes were dry and her expression was determined. "What now?" she asked, as if she hadn't just agreed to sign her life away. "We have two hours until we need to be at the bank."

"We'll find a coffee shop with free Wi-Fi so we can do some more research on Frankie Caruso. I also need to update my boss." He put the car in gear, backing carefully out of Gerald Ashton's driveway. At this moment, he didn't think he'd ever admired a woman more than he admired Rachel. She was beautiful, smart, sincere, and the one of the best mothers he'd ever known.

And the part of his heart that he'd sent into a deep freeze after Becky's and Sophie's deaths thawed just a little.

Rachel gratefully climbed out of the car at the coffee shop, hanging on to her new phone with a death grip. Nick purchased two large coffees and then found a small table near a gas fireplace. It was nice and cozy near the fire, and she sipped her coffee, gazing up at the wreath hanging above the mantel as he booted up the laptop.

"You can do some searching while I figure out a plan about handling the exchange," Nick said, turning the computer toward her. "Plus, I need to call a friend of mine to help with the exchange. Don't worry," he added, when he saw her dismay. "Jonah is someone I'd trust with my life. Unfortunately, we can't do this alone, Rachel. We need backup."

She nodded, her stomach twisting as she understood what he was saying. Getting the money from the bank was the easy part. Keeping her son alive during the exchange was going to be much tougher.

But failure was not an option.

As Nick made his calls, she sat there feeling numb. Even after he'd finished, she could only manage to stare blindly at the computer screen. For a moment she was tempted to start praying again. She regretted her harsh words to Nick earlier this morning. She'd been angry and had taken that anger out on him, wanting to hurt him the same way she was suffering.

Was she crazy to ask for God's help? Why would God listen to her? Her parents hadn't been religious, but she sensed they'd believed in God. At least they'd seemed to. Maybe she really was missing something important.

For a moment she bowed her head and opened her heart. *I'm sorry, Lord. I never should have said those hurtful things. Especially when they're not true. I know Nick believes in You and I want to believe, too. Please help show me the way. And please keep my son safe in Your care. Amen.*

As before, the moment she finished praying, a sense

of peace settled over her. She looked up and caught Nick staring at her, and she forced herself to smile. "I'm sorry, Nick. I do want to believe in God. I want to believe He'll keep Joey safe."

"I'm so glad, Rachel," he murmured, reaching over to take her hand in his. "Looks as if my prayers have been answered. I've been praying that you'd allow the Lord to help carry your burden."

Nick's hand was warm on hers, and she found it odd that she didn't want to let go. Never before had she ever depended on a man to help her. Except for her father, especially when she'd needed to escape Anthony. She knew she was lucky to have Nick's help with this. She never would have been able to manage alone.

Her new phone rang, interrupting the peaceful silence. Startled, she glanced at the screen, half expecting to see the familiar blocked call.

But the call was from Edith Goodman, her assistant. She winced as she realized she had forgotten to let Edith know she wouldn't be in the office today. Or at all, considering she wouldn't be the owner of the company once she returned from the bank in a few hours. "Hi, Edith," she said to her assistant. "I'm sorry I forgot to let you know that I'm taking the rest of the week off."

"The rest of the week?" Edith's voice rose sharply. "This isn't like you at all. What in the world is going on, Rachel?"

"I'm sorry, Edith, but there's something important I have to do." She wanted to reassure her assistant that Gerry would be there to take over the company, but Edith would find that out sooner or later. No need to spill the beans yet. "Just cancel my meetings and let everyone know I'm taking a personal leave of absence, okay?"

"If that's what you want," Edith replied slowly. "But

that wasn't the reason I called. I just thought you should know what happened, before you read about it in the newspaper."

"Read what?" She had no idea what her assistant was talking about. She hadn't even thought about reading the newspaper since getting the threatening notes. Surely there wasn't another pending lawsuit? She'd feel guilty selling her shares of stock to Gerry if in fact they weren't worth the price.

"Dr. Josie Gardener is dead, Rachel," Edith said, her voice tinged with sorrow. "It looks like she may have committed suicide late last night."

Nick knew that, whatever the contents of the phone call between Rachel and Edith, it was bad news. Rachel went pale, her fingers gripping the phone tightly as she listened.

"Do you know anything else?" she asked. He couldn't hear Edith's response, but then Rachel said, "Okay, thanks for letting me know," and she disconnected from the call.

"Rachel? What happened?" He took her hand in his, trying to offer some sort of comfort.

"One of my top research scientists was found dead in her home early this morning," she said in a whisper. "They think it might be a suicide."

Suicide? As before, the timing was too much of a coincidence. "Was this the same research scientist who was responsible for the new diabetes drug going to market and then being recalled by the FDA?" She nodded. "Josie Gardener wasn't the only one involved in creating the new medication. She worked with Dr. Karl Errol, too."

Nick glanced around, not wanting to discuss anything further in a public place. "Let's go out to the car," he murmured.

Rachel seemed to move in slow motion as they packed

up and went back outside, carrying their coffee. He felt better once they were safely settled in the car. "Is there any reason to suspect she was involved in covering up the side effects of the medication?"

"Of course not!" Rachel's denial was swift. "Her reputation was on the line with this new medication. And even if it wasn't, why commit suicide now? Why not back when the lawsuits were initially filed?"

She had a point, but he found he couldn't let it go. "Maybe she was afraid you'd find out the truth and couldn't bear to face the consequences of her actions?"

Rachel frowned for a moment, as if considering his idea. "I don't know, Nick. We have been working on releasing our research documents to the FDA, but if there was something Josie was trying to cover up, I'm sure Karl would have told me."

Unless Karl was in on it, too, he thought. Was it possible that Karl was responsible for kidnapping Joey? Maybe Karl's goal was to keep Rachel preoccupied while he swept the truth about the diabetes drug under the rug? Once he had the money, he could disappear out of the country without anyone being the wiser.

The more he thought about the theory, the more convinced he became that he was onto something. But he didn't think Rachel was going to go along with his idea—she was too loyal to her coworkers to think anything bad about them. "Where does Karl live?" he asked, trying to sound casual. "Maybe we should pay him a visit? See what he knows about Josie's death?"

"He lives in a small house not far from the company," Rachel said, her forehead wrinkled in a deep frown. "I would say he'd be at work, but, with Josie's death, I guess I'm not sure. They were close, but only in a professional way as far as I know. Neither one of them is married. Josie has a brother and a twin sister, but no children."

Nick felt bad for Josie's family, but he was more interested right now in where Karl Errol was. "Do you know Karl's home address?"

Rachel rattled it off as he entered it into his phone GPS. He pulled out of the coffee shop parking lot and followed the directions with a sense of grim determination. Hopefully, the good doctor would be at home, playing the role of grieving colleague.

When they pulled up in front of Karl Errol's house, the small, brick Tudor appeared to be deserted. There were no holiday decorations adorning the home, and the yard had a shaggy look of neglect beneath the light dusting of snow. "Stay here," he advised Rachel. "I'm going to take a look around outside."

"Should I call Edith and see if he's at the office?" she asked, as he slid out from behind the wheel.

"Sure." He flashed a reassuring smile before heading up the cracked sidewalk leading to the researcher's front door.

No response from inside the home, which was pretty much what he expected. He peered through the windows but couldn't see much—the sunlight outside caused a glare that made it difficult to see. He walked around the house, crunching on leaves as he made his way to the garage, which was closed and locked up tight. He strode over to the back door and checked it as well. The screen door opened, and his heart quickened as he tested the interior door.

Locked, but with a flimsy, old-fashioned type of lock. He considered trying to jimmy it with a credit card, but was loath to do anything illegal.

He hesitated on the cracked stoop. What if Joey was

inside the old house? What if his theory about Dr. Errol was right? That he'd kidnapped Joey to keep Rachel from uncovering his mistakes?

Wrestling with his conscience, he turned away from the door, but then caught sight of one of those fake rocks that were sometimes used to hide keys. Why people bothered with that sort of thing, he had no clue. Talk about being obvious. He reached down, opened up the fake rock and removed the key.

He accessed the house, wrinkling his nose at the stale air. When was the last time the doctor had been home? Either the guy simply lived like this, or he was holed up somewhere else—with Joey—biding his time until he could get his hands on Rachel's cash.

He quickly swept through the house, including the up-stairs bedrooms but didn't find anything suspicious. There were only three bedrooms, and they were all empty. He even went down in the basement, which was dark and dank, smelling strongly of mold.

Nothing. Which he found a bit odd. Usually people left a bit of themselves strewn around, at least a bill or a coupon or something. But the place was so void of any-thing personal that he couldn't help wondering if he was on the right track. Granted, he hadn't found Joey here, but he wasn't willing to give up his theory just yet.

Back up in the kitchen, he searched for notes or any-thing at all that might indicate where Dr. Errol had gone. The garbage can was empty and there wasn't a single stray note to be found. He even went back to the master bedroom, but still didn't find anything.

Dr. Errol was either innocent or smarter than he'd given the guy credit for. And he was leaning toward the latter.

He left the house the same way he'd come in, return-
ng the key to its hiding place in the fake rock. He hur-

ried back around to the front, where Rachel was waiting in the car.

"What took you so long?" she asked, when he slid in behind the wheel. "I was getting ready to come out and look for you."

"Sorry, I was poking around and lost track of time. Did you get in touch with Edith?"

"Yes, she said that Karl called in saying he was staying home today." She stared at the house through the windshield. "Maybe we should try knocking at the door again?"

Time to come clean. "Actually, I found the house key hidden in a rock near the back door. I went in and checked out the house. Believe me, no one is home. And from what I saw, I don't think he's been home in a couple of days, either."

"He hasn't been home?" She stared at him incredulously. "But that's crazy. I know for a fact that Karl was at work the day we met in my office. I had a meeting scheduled with both him and Josie that I canceled."

"That was on Wednesday," he said thoughtfully, going back through the timeline. It was Thursday and he found it hard to believe that only twenty-four hours had passed since he'd sat in Rachel's office looking at the threatening notes she'd received. "That means he must have been planning this for a while."

"You don't know what you're talking about," Rachel said, crossing her arms over her chest. "I saw the guy who kidnapped Joey, remember? He was young, in his late twenties or early thirties. I can guarantee he wasn't Karl Errol. Karl is a short, rather nerdy type of guy with glasses and a half-bald head, although I don't think he's hit the age of forty yet."

She was clearly exasperated with him, but he couldn't just let this go "Rachel, it's best if we keep all possibilities open, okay? Errol could have easily hired Morales to kidnap Joey."

"Believe what you want," she said with a disgusted sigh. "I know that Karl isn't capable of doing anything like this."

There was no point in continuing the argument, so he concentrated on backing out of the driveway and heading back toward the city. They still had a good hour and fifteen minutes before they were due at the bank.

However, Rachel wouldn't drop the subject, even though he hadn't said a word. "Obviously you've forgotten how we were shot at outside Margie Caruso's house, which implicates the Mafia, not one of my employees."

He hadn't forgotten, but that incident had been more of a warning rather than an attempt to kill them. "Maybe we should head back over there, then?" he asked. "We have time."

"Great idea," she agreed enthusiastically.

He stifled a sigh and headed toward the freeway. They'd driven about twenty minutes when Rachel's cell phone beeped. He tightened his grip on the steering wheel because so far the only person who'd texted Rachel since this nightmare began was the kidnapper.

"He wants to know if I have the money yet," Rachel said, glancing up nervously. "What should I tell him?"

"Tell him that we'll have the money by one o'clock this afternoon. That gives us a little bit of a buffer since we're hoping to have this settled by noon."

"I don't know if that's a good idea," she protested. "I don't want to make him angry."

Nick understood her concern, but he wanted some time to react to the kidnapper's exchange plan. Since Logan was out of the country, he'd had no choice but to call his friend and fellow cop, Jonah Stewart, for assistance. Jonah lived with his wife, Mallory, in Milwaukee, but once he'd heard the story, Jonah had readily agreed to drive up to Chicago. "If this guy understands anything about banks, he'll understand the time frame is more than reasonable."

Rachel swallowed hard and sent the message explaining they'd have the money by one o'clock in the afternoon.

There was a tense silence as she waited for the kidnapper's response. When her phone beeped again, she picked it up with shaking fingers.

"Well?" he asked. "What was his response?"

Rachel lifted her tormented gaze to his, her lower lip quivering with fear. "He said to text him the minute we get the money and not a second later. He also said he'd hurt Joey and keep on hurting him for every minute we're late."

SEVEN

Rachel shivered, despite the bright sunlight streaming in through the windshield keeping the interior of the car toasty warm. She couldn't bear the thought of the kidnapper hurting her son. She didn't even want to think about what Joey may have already suffered.

She forced her frozen fingers to text back. I promise I'll call as soon as I have the cash. Please don't harm my son.

"Rachel, try not to panic. I'm sure he's bluffing," Nick murmured, reaching over to squeeze her hand.

"I'm not willing to take that chance," she snapped.

Nick didn't seem a bit fazed by her anger. "Remember, we've just purchased a new phone. There's no way for him to track us from now on. And it could be that he isn't even aware of that fact, yet."

Suddenly, the idea of getting a new phone didn't seem like such a good one. Her heart lodged in her throat and she gripped his hand tightly. "What if he gets mad about the switch and hurts Joey?"

"Don't worry, Rachel," Nick said in a soothing tone. "The kidnapper has come too far to turn back now. He wants your money, remember?"

Nick's theory wasn't at all reassuring. Yes, the kidnapper wanted her money, but it could be that he also had a sadistic streak and took some kind of perverse pleasure from hurting young children, too. She was tempted to beg Nick to return to the truck stop, so she could grab her old phone out of the garbage.

But he was already heading down the highway toward Margie Caruso's house, so she bit her tongue and tried to relax. At least for now, the kidnapper couldn't track their movements, which was a good thing. She hoped and prayed that they'd find Joey there.

This time, Nick didn't pull up in front of the house, but drove around the block, parking on the opposite side of the house. It was broad daylight, so it wasn't exactly easy to hide from curious eyes.

"Remember, I'm the one who's going to do the talking here," she reminded Nick as they slid out of the car.

He grimaced and nodded, keeping a sharp eye out as they walked down the street. Margie Caruso's house was the third one in from the corner, so it didn't take long to get there.

She could hear the faint hint of Christmas music coming from one of the houses, and she couldn't help quickening her pace, eager to see if Margie was home. Nick hung back as she walked up the sidewalk and rang the doorbell.

The seconds passed with agonizing slowness, but soon the door opened, revealing a well-dressed and nicely groomed woman who didn't look anything close to her fifty-some years. But the moment Margie saw Rachel standing there, she frowned. "No soliciting," she said abruptly.

"Wait! My name is Rachel Caruso. I'm not selling anything, I just want to talk to you for a minute."

Margie paused in the act of closing the door, her gaze raking over Rachel from head to toe. "You're Anthony's wife?" she asked.

Hiding a wince, she nodded. She tried to think of a way to forge a bond with the woman. "We divorced a long time ago, but I was hoping you wouldn't mind talking to me for a few minutes."

The former Mrs. Frankie Caruso pursed her lips for a moment. "Who's he?" she asked, gesturing toward Nick.

"This is Nick, a good friend of mine." She twisted her hands together, hoping Margie wouldn't guess that he was a cop and refuse to see them. Rachel didn't exactly want to have this conversation outside. Not that she was even sure what she was going to say. The main reason they'd come to Margie's house was to make sure Joey wasn't being held here.

"I guess you'd better come in, then," Margie said, opening the screen door for them.

Nick held the door as she entered the house first. She glanced around curiously and was a little disheartened to find nothing unusual. There were some holiday decorations, including a small fake tabletop-size tree. Would Margie invite her in if she was hiding her son here? Somehow she doubted it. Yet she firmly believed Margie Caruso would be a link to her son. "You have a very nice home," she murmured as she stepped into the living room.

Margie let out a bark of laughter. "Yep. Bought and paid for by Frankie," she bragged. "Do you want something to drink? I have coffee and soft drinks."

"No thanks. I really hope you don't mind us just dropping in like this," she said, before Nick could respond. "It's just I need to find Frankie and I was hoping you'd know where he was."

"Have a seat," Margie said, waving at them as she dropped into a recliner. "What do you want with Frankie?"

Rachel's mouth went dry and she wished she'd agreed

to take something to drink. "It's nothing major, I just need to ask him a few questions."

"Ms. Caruso, do you mind if I use your bathroom?" Nick asked, interrupting them.

"No problem, it's down the hall to your right," Margie said, waving in the general direction.

Rachel figured Nick was trying to give them some time alone, most likely thinking that Margie might open up more if he wasn't sitting there. She stared down at her hands for a minute trying to figure out a way to get Margie to speak openly about Frankie. "Last I heard, Frankie was in Phoenix," she said in a low voice. "I should tell you that I've received some threatening letters and phone calls." She glanced up, trying to assess Margie's reaction. "I guess I couldn't help wondering if your ex might be involved."

Margie let out a sigh. "I highly doubt Frankie's entangled in something like that," she said without hesitation. "It's not really his style."

"What is his style?" Rachel pressed. "I divorced Anthony a long time ago, so how do I know Frankie's not holding some sort of grudge against me?"

Margie tapped one long, lacquered nail against the end table. "Frankie has been splitting his time between Phoenix and Chicago, but I can't imagine he's holding the divorce against you. Why would he? Our divorce wasn't that big of a deal."

The news that Frankie Caruso could be right now in Chicago made her pulse race with a mixture of dread and excitement. Frankie had to be the one behind Joey's kidnapping…it was the only thing that made sense. "I have to tell you, I admired how you and Frankie seemed to get along, even after your divorce," Rachel said.

"Yes, well, we had some business ventures together,

which helped," Margie replied evasively. Rachel tried not to show her distaste—certainly, those business ventures were likely Mafia related.

"Like I said, it's just amazing that you both managed to stay friends," Rachel added. "Obviously, that wasn't exactly the case with me and Anthony."

"I know. Anthony wasn't shy about telling us how upset he was at how you managed to keep him from your son." Margie's gaze was challenging, as if daring Rachel to disagree.

The mention of Joey kicked her pulse into high gear. So Frankie and Margie knew about Joey. Knew that she'd kept Anthony away from his son. Was this the motive behind the kidnapping? A way to show her the power of the Caruso name?

"Me and Frankie didn't have kids," Margie continued, clearly oblivious to Rachel's spinning thoughts. "I guess it was a good thing, considering how we didn't stay together."

Rachel couldn't decide if Margie was putting on an act for her benefit or not. She didn't dare glance at her watch, even though Nick had been gone for what seemed like a really long time. She didn't want Margie to wonder where he was, either. "I guess maybe you're right," she murmured. "Divorce is much easier without fighting over kids." Before the other woman could ask anything more, Rachel quickly changed the subject. "Are you going to see Frankie anytime soon?"

Margie's eyebrows lifted. "Maybe. Why?"

Flustered, Rachel strove to keep her tone light and casual. "I thought maybe you could just mention to him that I'd like to talk to him. If he has some time. Nothing urgent…"

Margie stared at her for a long moment, as if trying to

gauge what Rachel really wanted. "Yeah, sure. I might see him. Maybe you should give me your phone number so that he has it if he wants to get in touch with you."

"Of course. Do you have a pen and paper handy?"

Margie rose to her feet at the same moment Nick walked back into the room. "Wait here for a minute."

After their hostess left the room, she looked at Nick. "Well?" she asked in a low voice.

"Nothing," he murmured with a slight shake of his head.

Nothing, as in he didn't get to search very much? Or nothing, as in he truly hadn't found anything?

Before she could ask anything more, Margie returned. Rachel hastily scribbled her number on the slip of paper the older woman handed her. "Thanks so much, Margie. I really appreciate you taking the time to talk to me."

"No problem." Margie walked them to the front door. "Take care."

"You, too," Rachel said, before slipping outside. Nick followed her, grabbing her hand as they strolled down the sidewalk to the street. "We probably shouldn't have parked far away," she murmured under her breath. "Margie will think it's odd that we didn't pull up right in front of her house."

"You might be right," Nick said. "But you did a good job of convincing her that your reason for being there was related to Frankie. Maybe she'll think we're just paranoid."

Once they turned the corner, Rachel relaxed. "I *was* there because of Frankie. He's been here in Chicago, Nick. I think he must be involved in Joey's kidnapping."

Nick didn't say anything more until they were in the car. "Frankie might be involved, but as far as I could tell, Margie isn't. I looked around and didn't find anything. I even managed to sneak down the basement stairs. There weren't any hiding places down there that I could see, so I didn't spend a lot of time searching. I was afraid she'd hear me."

Rachel couldn't believe he'd managed to get all the way into the basement. "What would you have done if she had heard you?" she demanded.

He shrugged. "I would have claimed that I took a wrong turn."

She put a hand over her knotted stomach, glad she hadn't known what Nick was doing while she chatted with Margie. Her nerves were already at the breaking point. Time was running out; they were due to be at the bank in the next twenty minutes.

Soon, they'd be one step closer to getting Joey back, safe and sound.

Nick glanced at Rachel as he navigated the traffic, taking the fastest route to the bank. He couldn't say he was surprised that they hadn't found anything at Margie Caruso's house. He still believed that Dr. Karl Errol might be the missing link. But no matter what he thought, there wasn't enough time to keep searching for Joey. He knew that once they'd finished their transaction at the bank, Rachel would contact the kidnapper.

There was no way she'd risk anything happening to her son. Not that he could blame her. Easy for him to say the kidnapper was bluffing. If Rachel found a single mark on Joey, she'd never forgive him.

His phone rang and he picked it up, recognizing Jonah Stewart's number. "Hey, are you in town?"

"Yep, sitting in the parking lot of the hotel down the road from the bank."

Nick could feel Rachel's curious gaze on him. "Good.

We'll be at the bank within the next ten minutes or so. I'll be in touch as soon as we're finished."

"Sounds good. I'll be waiting."

"Thanks, buddy." He disconnected from the call.

"Was that the cop buddy you told me about?" Rachel asked.

"Yeah, Jonah Stewart is a Milwaukee detective who helped build a case against your ex-husband. Anthony tried to kill him. Thankfully, Jonah and Mallory escaped, and Anthony was the one who'd died that night."

"So he was the one responsible for bringing down Anthony," Rachel mused. "I always wondered exactly what happened."

The last thing he wanted was for Rachel to hear the gory details. "None of that matters now. Just know that we really can trust Jonah."

Rachel nodded and looked away, staring out the window as if lost in thought.

He mentally kicked himself for reminding her of Anthony Caruso, especially at a time like this, when her son was still missing. Didn't she already have enough to worry about? Right now, she needed to stay focused on the task of getting the money together. That was the first step. The second was to exchange the money for her son.

With the kidnapper calling the shots, they'd be lucky to get Joey back without incident, even with Jonah's help. "Nick?"

He dragged his gaze to meet Rachel's. "Yes?"

"I want you to promise me something."

Uh-oh. He braced himself, certain he wasn't going to like this. "Promise you what?"

She locked eyes with him. "Promise me that you'll get Joey out of there safely. I don't want you to worry about me—I want you to focus on keeping my son safe."

Every instinct in his body protested, but he knew very well that if the situation was reversed, he'd ask the exact same thing. Children were a cherished gift from God and they deserved a chance to be protected. As much as he didn't want to lose Rachel, he knew he had to give her this much.

"I promise," he vowed, silently asking God to spare both Rachel and Joey so he wouldn't be forced to make an impossible choice.

Rachel rubbed her sweaty palms on the sides of her jeans before picking up the pen to sign over her shares of the company stock to Gerry Ashton. She couldn't help glancing at her watch, wondering if right now, the kidnapper was somewhere close watching them.

"Are you sure about this, Rachel?" Edward Callahan asked. The poor bank manager had been beside himself since they'd arrived. She wanted to believe he cared about her, but she suspected the large withdrawal of cash was the main source of his concern.

"Absolutely." She wasn't nervous about selling off her company; she was worried about Joey. Because the moment Edward handed over the cash, she'd have to call the kidnappers.

Please, Lord, please don't let them hurt my son.

The transaction was completed with ridiculous simplicity—she was sure she'd completed far more paperwork when she'd bought her house eight years ago.

A house that she'd have to sell, once she had her son back. She shoved the thoughts away, refusing to dwell on her decision. She'd give up everything she owned to get Joey back.

"I have the cash pulled together in the vault," Edward said as Gerry finished his portion of the agreement. "It wasn't easy… I had to send couriers to several other branches to get what you needed. I—uh, put it all in a large duffel bag for you. I didn't want it to look too obvious as you left the building. A cashier's check would be much safer," he added, even though he'd already lectured her on the perils of walking around with so much money.

"I know, thanks, Edward." She forced a smile as she turned toward Gerry. "I haven't told anyone at the office yet, but I'd appreciate it if you'd tell Edith first, privately."

Gerry's forehead was puckered in a concerned frown. "I will. Rachel, I wish there was more I could do to help you…."

"You've helped more than you could ever know," she assured him. "Thanks again."

Gerry gave her a quick hug and then tucked his copy of the paperwork into his briefcase and made his way toward the door. She turned her attention toward the bank manager. "I'm ready."

Nick stayed close at her side as they walked into the bank vault. Edward used his ID to open the first door and then punched in a key to access the second door. Once inside the vault, she saw the duffel bag he'd mentioned, surprised to find that it was the size of a small suitcase.

"I promise it's all there," Edward said, as she opened the bag and went through the contents. She'd never seen so much money before, especially not such crisp one-thousand-dollar bills.

"I'm sure you'll understand Rachel's need to verify the amount," Nick said, standing over her as if worried the bank manager himself was in on the kidnapping.

"Of course," Edward agreed, discreetly wiping more sweat from his brow.

She focused on the task at hand. The thousand-dollar bills were bound in stacks of one hundred so it didn't take long to validate the amount was correct. "Thanks again, Edward," she said, as she rose to her feet, slinging the duffel bag strap over her shoulder.

"We'd like to leave through the back door," Nick announced.

Edward nodded and led the way back out the vault, pausing long enough to close and lock both doors before he took them to the back of the bank.

Nick stayed close to her side as they left the building and climbed back into the car. She crammed the duffel bag on the floor between her feet, too afraid to store it in the backseat. The minute they were settled, she pulled out her phone.

"Wait just a minute, okay?" Nick said, putting a hand on her arm. "Let me call Jonah first."

The image of her son being hurt was impossible to ignore. It took every ounce of willpower for her to wait for Nick to call Jonah. He hadn't even completed his call when she quickly texted the kidnapper, I have the money.

Within seconds, her phone rang. Before she could push the button to answer, Nick whispered, "Put the call on speaker."

With trembling fingers she did as he directed. "This is Rachel."

"Go to the abandoned barn located twenty miles outside the city near the intersection of Highway F and Highway 93 in exactly one hour," the mechanically distorted voice directed. "Come alone or your son will pay the price."

Rachel swallowed hard. "I'll be there," she whispered, never doubting for one moment the kidnapper would make good on his threat.

If he hadn't hurt Joey already.

EIGHT

Nick watched the blood drain from Rachel's face, leaving her pale and shaking. He wanted nothing more than to take her into his arms and offer comfort, but this wasn't the time or the place. Right now, they had to get to the abandoned barn as soon as possible, if they were going to be successful in getting Joey back.

He called Jonah, repeating the kidnapper's directives. "I'm not sure where this place is, but we need to take only one car, as it doesn't sound like there's a lot of cover," he told his friend. "And, if you don't mind, it might be best if we take your car to change it up a bit. Rachel and I have been driving around town in mine, and the kidnappers might recognize it. What do you think, buddy?"

"Sounds good." Jonah quickly gave him directions to where he was parked at his hotel on the edge of town and they agreed to meet there in less than ten minutes.

"It's almost over, Rachel," he said, reaching out to squeeze her hand before he put the car in gear and drove away from the bank. "We're going to get Joey back."

"I'm so scared," she whispered. "There are so many things that could go wrong."

"Try not to think of the worst-case scenario," he advised, knowing that was his job.

"I won't. But I'll be glad when this is over."

He didn't bother pointing out that even if they managed to get Joey back unharmed, the nightmare might not be over. There was no guarantee the kidnapper would simply disappear once this exchange was completed. Especially since Morales was nothing more than a hired thug, doing what he was told. Whether the source of the kidnapping was the Mafia or someone related to her company, Rachel and Joey could still be in danger.

And of the two scenarios, he still found himself leaning toward the possibility that this was all somehow connected to her company.

He slowly unclenched his hands from the steering wheel. He needed to keep a cool head. Right now, it was best to focus on the upcoming swap. Later, there would be plenty of time to think about who was behind this.

The moment he pulled into the hotel parking lot, they quickly switched vehicles. Rachel lugged the duffel bag of money and Jonah handed the keys to Nick, choosing to climb into the backseat.

Nick quickly introduced the two and then started the engine. "Pleased to meet you, Rachel," Jonah Stewart said as he buckled himself in.

Rachel tried to smile, but it wasn't much of one. "Thanks for helping us."

"I don't mind at all. We're going to get your son back, Ms. Simon," Jonah said reassuringly.

"Please, call me Rachel."

Nick listened to their brief conversation as he drove, pushing the speed limit as much as he dared while following the directions leading them to the designated meeting spot. The GPS took them directly out of town, into farm country. As the traffic thinned, he pushed his speed even further, wanting to make good time.

The kidnapper hadn't chosen the location or the tight timeline by accident. Clearly the guy didn't want to give them too much time to prepare. And Nick absolutely didn't want to get there after the kidnappers were already there. He was hoping that the perpetrators might have to pick up Joey first, before meeting them, which would give them the time they needed.

A half hour would be nice, but he'd take less time if he had to. They would need every second to get the lay of the land. And to get Jonah hidden someplace nearby where no one would see him.

"Dear Lord, please keep my son safe in Your care," Rachel whispered.

Her quiet prayer caught him off guard, but he quickly joined in. "And, Lord, please guide us and give us strength as we fight to get Joey back safe and sound."

"Amen," Jonah said from the backseat. Rachel glanced over her shoulder at Jonah in surprise.

Nick reached over and squeezed her hand. "Jonah is a believer, too."

"Good to know," she said in a soft voice. "I feel like I need all the help we can get." There was a slight pause before she asked, "Does praying always make you feel calmer?"

"Absolutely," he agreed. "Sharing my burdens with God always helps me feel better."

"I wish I knew more about God and faith and prayer," Rachel said. "I feel like I'm not worthy of His help."

"You are worthy, Rachel, and so is Joey. But if you'd really like to learn more, I'd be honored to teach you." He didn't want to push her too hard, but he was thrilled that she had opened her heart and her soul to God and faith. "Once we have Joey back, I'll be happy to study the Bible with you."

"After we have Joey back," Rachel repeated. "I'm going to hold you to that, Nick." She was twisting her hands together in the way he knew meant she was worrying again.

"We're going to be okay, Rachel," Jonah chimed in from the backseat. "God will guide us through this. We've been in other tight spots before, right, Nick?"

"Right," Nick agreed drily.

There was so much more he wanted to say, but off in the distance he caught sight of an abandoned barn at the end of what looked to be a hard-packed dirt road. That must be the meeting place. His heart sank as he realized it was out in the middle of a wide-open space, where it would be difficult to hide any backup.

"Take a look, Jonah," he said, gesturing toward the barn. "They sure didn't leave us many options."

"We'll find something," Jonah replied with confidence. "I doubt they're going to take the time to search the entire barn. I suspect they'll make this a quick exchange and get out of Dodge."

"I hope you're right," Nick muttered, pushing down harder on the accelerator. He couldn't help constantly looking at the clock on Jonah's dashboard. It seemed that time was slipping away from them.

The kidnappers would be there in forty-two minutes. Unless, of course, they decided to show up early. In that case, there was no way to judge how much time they had to prepare.

Rachel's stomach hurt so badly she feared she might be sick. She took several deep breaths and wrapped her arms tightly across her middle. She could do this.

She had to do this.

The big dilapidated barn loomed ominously as they approached. This was it. The moment she'd been waiting for and dreading at the same time. In less than forty minutes the kidnappers would drive up with her son, demanding money in exchange for his freedom.

Please, Lord, please keep Joey safe!

The calm she'd felt before after praying seemed to have deserted her now. Maybe because her prayers betrayed the depth of her desperation. Despite Nick's reassurances that she was worthy, she couldn't help feeling that maybe God thought she was a big fraud. But she hoped He wouldn't punish her son for her previous lack of faith. She took another deep breath.

Nick backed up the dirt road so that the car was facing outward toward the road. The minute he shut off the car, he and Jonah jumped out to see what they had to work with.

She was still trying to pull herself together. But when she stared down at the duffel bag, she realized she couldn't sit here. She had to be in the driver's seat, as if she'd just driven here by herself. Swallowing hard, she shoved open the door, hauled the duffel bag up so that it was on the seat, and then slammed the door.

Nick had Jonah's car keys, so she went to find him. She needed the kidnappers to believe she'd followed their instructions to the letter.

The barn door was open only about a foot, so she turned sideways to slide inside. The interior was surprisingly dim. She's expected it to be brighter considering there were several missing boards and glassless windows. The place reeked of fertilizer mixed with musty old hay, thanks to the piles that looked as if they'd been there untouched for years.

Nick stood, looking up at the loft. She followed his gaze and gasped when she saw Jonah carefully going up a rickety old ladder that didn't look strong enough to hold his weight.

"Are you sure that's safe?" she whispered.

"Not really, but he insisted on giving it a try."

There was a loud noise as Jonah's foot broke through one of the rungs of the ladder. Her heart lodged in her throat as he hung there for a moment before he regained his balance. In a few minutes, Jonah was safely on the loft.

"Wouldn't he be better off down here?" She couldn't imagine the rotted wood that made up the loft floor would be any sturdier than the ladder.

"I'll be down on the ground level, and he's going to try and get some leverage from up above. See that window up there?" He indicated the open space in the wall of the barn located above the loft. "It overlooks the front of the barn, and that's our best option."

She felt dizzy watching Jonah ease his way into position, so she lowered her gaze and tried not to sneeze. Despite the cold December air, the moldy hay was making her eyes water. "Where are you planning to be?"

"Outside, as close to you as I can manage," he said grimly. "There are several stacks of hay outside along the north side of the barn. If I drag a few more out there, I should be fairly well hidden."

She helped Nick carry a couple of stacks of smelly, musty hay outside. They had to open the barn door wider and it groaned loudly in protest. She froze, hoping it wouldn't fall off.

After two trips, they had a decent-size stack of hay along the side of the barn. Nick carefully closed the barn door and then used a bunch of hay like a broom to brush the dirt, covering up their footprints.

The north side of the barn seemed too far away for her piece of mind, but she bit her lip so that she wouldn't complain. After all, she couldn't very well expect Nick to hide in the backseat of Jonah's car. Truthfully, she was lucky to have any backup at all.

"You might want to give me the car keys, just in case they want me to go someplace else," she said.

Nick scowled and dug them out of the front pocket of his jeans. "Here you go. But don't follow those guys someplace else, Rachel. There would be nothing to prevent them from killing both you and Joey, while still taking off with the cash. Your best option is to stay right here, where Jonah and I can protect you."

"I know," she said, taking the keys from Nick. As much as she knew he was right, she wasn't sure she'd be able to say no if it came to the kidnappers giving her an ultimatum. Her greatest weakness was her son's safety. If they threatened to hurt him, she knew she'd go along with whatever they asked of her.

She turned to walk away, but suddenly Nick grabbed her hand to stop her. Glancing over her shoulder, she found him staring at her intently. "What's wrong?" she asked.

"Nothing. Just—be careful, okay?" he said gruffly. Then, before she could respond, he pulled her close and gave her a quick kiss.

The kiss was over before she had a chance to register what had happened. But she longed to throw herself into his arms, absorbing some of his strength. This wasn't the time or the place, though, so she said the first thing that came to mind. "Remember your promise," she blurted. "No matter what happens, save my son."

He stared at her for a long moment. "I won't forget my promise, Rachel. But my goal is to get both of you out of here safely." He turned away and began digging a hole for himself in the hay.

She turned and hurried back to the car. By the time

she'd slid into the driver's seat, she couldn't hear him any longer. He must have gotten himself hidden very quickly.

Her lips tingled and she wondered if Nick had kissed her on purpose to distract her. If so, his ruse had worked. For a couple of minutes her stomach hadn't hurt, although now the pain was back with a vengeance. She took another deep breath and focused on the task at hand, anxious to be ready if the kidnappers showed up early.

The driver's seat was all wrong, so she scooted the seat up so that she could reach the pedals and adjusted the mirrors to accommodate her smaller frame. From the way Nick had parked the car, she couldn't see much of the north side of the barn, which was back and to her left. Using the rearview mirror, she could just barely catch a portion of the stacked hay.

Nick and Jonah were both armed and ready. She tried to find comfort in the fact that if she couldn't see Jonah or Nick, then the kidnappers couldn't see them, either.

The minutes ticked by with excruciating slowness, and she resisted the urge to turn on the car to warm up. If she was cold, surely Jonah and Nick were even more so.

Within five minutes of waiting, she spotted a black Jeep coming down the highway from the same direction they'd come. With a frown, she followed the Jeep's progress. If this one belonged to the kidnappers, they were fifteen minutes early.

Rachel clutched the steering wheel and strained her eyes in an attempt to catch a glimpse of her son. She thought there might be someone in the passenger seat, but the Jeep was too far away to be certain.

At the last possible moment, the Jeep slowed and then turned onto the dirt road. She held her breath as the vehicle approached. The driver was the same big dark-haired man who'd snatched Joey out from the car crash. There was a smaller person in the passenger seat and when the Jeep came closer, she could tell the small person had a dark hood over his head. The Jeep pulled to a stop about thirty feet from her vehicle.

Panic threatened to overwhelm her. What if the person in the front seat really wasn't Joey? What if this was nothing more than a horrible trick? What if they planned to kill her and take the money, while keeping her son to sell him in the black market of human trafficking?

Her pulse thundered in her ears as she pushed open the car door. She grabbed the duffel bag of money and dragged it over the console so that it was right next to her, as she stepped out of the car.

"I want to see my son!" she said in a loud voice.

The driver, who had to be Morales, reached over and yanked the hood off her son's head. Joey squinted and ducked his head, shying away from the light. He reminded her of a prisoner who'd been locked in a cell for days, unable to bear normal daylight.

Cold fury swamped her. It was all she could do not to rush over to grab Joey and yank him out of there. She narrowed her gaze and stared, waiting for direction.

Morales slowly and deliberately pushed open his door and stood. Her heart dropped to the soles of her feet when he leveled his gun directly at her son. "One wrong move, lady, and I'll shoot to kill."

"I have the money," she blurted out. "You can have it. All I want is my son."

"Hold on, now," he said, sweeping his gaze around the area. She never flinched, trusting the men behind her to stay well hidden. "You'll get your kid soon enough."

"I'm not armed and I'm here alone, just like you asked," she said, drawing his attention back to her. "Here's the money. If you'll just let Joey out of the car, we'll make the swap."

His expression turned ugly. "Listen here, lady, *I'm* the one who's in charge. The kid doesn't move until I say so."

Her fingers clenched on the duffel bag as the seconds drew out to a full minute. He approached her with slow, deliberate steps, rounding the front of the Jeep. With every step closer, she grew more nervous. She came out from behind the safety of the driver's door, lugging the duffel bag.

"Set it down, where I can see it," he said in a low, guttural voice. So far, his movements had been slow and cautious, but the glint of excitement in his eyes betrayed his greed.

Ironically, that glimpse was enough to make her relax. She was certain he wasn't going to do anything foolish if that meant risking the money. But she didn't set the duffel bag down the way he told her to. "I will, but only if you let Joey open his car door."

He glared at her for a minute before giving a little wave of the gun. "Open your door, kid, nice and easy."

She tried not to divert her attention from the gunman, but she couldn't help sneaking a sideways glance at Joey. He was still squinting, as if he couldn't see very well but managed to open his passenger-side door. She could see his feet dangling outside the car, in the familiar basketball shoes she'd bought for him earlier in the school year. They were bright orange, his favorite color, and her eyes stung with the memory of how excited he'd been when he'd worn them for the first time.

The Jeep was high off the ground, and she wanted to call out a warning to Joey to be careful. But with the gunman so close, she didn't dare. Instead, she opened the duffel bag, holding it awkwardly against her chest, to show him the cash inside.

The gleam in his eyes got brighter, and she was struck by the fact that this guy obviously wasn't very smart. Nick was right—there had to be someone else acting as the brains of this operation. Morales was nothing more than a pawn. Right now, though, all she cared about was her son.

"Get out of the car, kid," Morales shouted. When she glanced over at her son, the thug lunged forward in an attempt to grab the money, but Rachel was faster. She snatched the handles of the bag, whipped it around and threw it at Morales, hitting him directly in the chest. "Run, Joey!"

While Morales was grappling with the bag, trying to make sure he didn't lose any of the cash, she leaped forward and grabbed her son. With a herculean effort, she hauled him up and ran toward the car, using her body to protect him as best she could. "Get inside," she urged.

"Stop!" Morales shouted. The sound of gunfire erupted and she ducked behind the open driver's door and threw herself over Joey, squashing him against the front seat.

"Stay down!" Nick shouted, coming around the corner of the barn, looking like a madman with straw sticking out of his hair and clinging to his clothes.

Morales turned and fired again. Panic-stricken, she glanced sideways and caught a glimpse of Nick hitting the ground. "Nick!" she screamed.

More gunfire, this time from up above, but Morales had already thrown the duffel into his Jeep and taken off, his tires churning up clouds of dust as he barreled down the dirt road.

NINE

Nick ignored the burning pain in his left arm as he crawled across the ground to reach Rachel and Joey. She held her son in a tight hug as if she might never let him go. Every instinct in his body was clamoring for him to follow Morales, but he couldn't bring himself to leave Rachel and her son. Or take them along, putting them in more danger.

"Are you all right?" he asked, pulling himself upright and leaning against the car. "Any injuries?"

"No injuries," Rachel murmured as she lifted her tear-streaked face from her son's hair. She barely glanced at Nick, her attention focused solely on her son. She brushed his hair away from his forehead. "Joey? Are you sure you're not hurt anywhere?"

Joey shook his head but didn't say anything, burrowing his face once again against his mother. The boy's silence was a bit concerning, but not completely unexpected considering the trauma he'd been through.

"Nick, you're bleeding!" Rachel reached out to touch his arm. "He hit you?"

"Winged by a bullet, nothing serious," he said, glancing around for Jonah. His buddy shoved open the barn door and came out, limping.

"I tried to take out the Jeep, but I fell through a hole in the floor," Jonah said with disgust. "I'm sorry I let him get away."

"Nothing more you could have done, Jonah," Nick assured his friend. "And the way you shot at him from up in the loft obviously scared him off, which is probably a good thing. He was armed, and the way things were going down, I doubt he intended to leave any witnesses once he got the cash."

"Yeah, I got that same feeling," Jonah muttered. He looked at his car and scowled, fingering the bullet hole in the back door along the driver's side. "Now I know why you wanted me to take my car. Hope he didn't hit anything in the engine."

The bullet holes in the back door of the driver's side were sobering, proof of how lucky they were to get out of this with a gouge in his arm and nothing more serious. "I'll reimburse you, Jonah."

"No biggie," his friend said, waving him off. Joey lifted his head and gazed at both him and Jonah with suspicion. Nick belatedly realized they were both strangers to the child, so he dropped to his knees and smiled over at the boy. "Hi, Joey, my name is Nick Butler and I'm a detective with the Chicago Police Department. And that's my buddy Jonah Stewart, who is a police detective, too, from Milwaukee. We've been helping your mom find you."

"Thank you," Joey said in a wobbly voice, his curiosity apparently satisfied. "Can we go home now? I'm hungry."

Nick was trying to figure out a way to let the boy know it wasn't safe to go home yet, when Rachel interrupted. "You're hungry? Did they give you anything to eat or drink?"

Joey shook his head. "No. They kept me in a room in the basement. It was dark and I think there were big hairy spiders, too. The door was locked and I had a mattress and a toilet but nothing else," he admitted, his lower lip trembling with the effort not to cry.

Rachel's eyes filled with tears. "I'm so sorry, Joey. So sorry…" Once again, she hugged him close as if she could erase the horrible memories by will alone.

"We'd better get out of here," Jonah said quietly. "In case they decide to come back."

Nick couldn't agree more. "Rachel, do you have the car keys?"

She sniffled and used the sleeve of her jacket to wipe away her tears. "Here you go," she said as she handed them over. "Joey and I will take the backseat."

He understood she couldn't bear to let go of her son. "You'd better drive," Nick told Jonah, as he loped around to the passenger side of the vehicle. "I'm going to call my boss and put an APB out on that Jeep. And I don't suppose you have a first-aid kit in here somewhere?"

"In the glove box," Jonah said. He slid behind the wheel and grunted as his knees hit the steering wheel. He adjusted the seat back and then started the car.

Nick called Ryan Walsh, quickly filling his captain in on the details. "I'm fairly certain the driver was Ricky Morales and the Jeep's tag number is JVW-555."

Walsh wasn't entirely thrilled to hear what had transpired. "I'm glad you got the kid back, but we need to keep looking for the link to the Mafia," he said. "When are you coming in to file your report?"

"Soon," Nick hedged. "Just let me know as soon as you hear anything about Morales or the Jeep, okay?" He disconnected from the call.

"Where to?" Jonah asked, as he turned off the dirt road and back onto the highway.

"That's a good question," Nick muttered, as he rummaged around for the first-aid kit. "We should probably pick up my car first."

"No, we need to stop for something to eat, first," Rachel said from the backseat. "Joey's hungry."

"Is he all right? Or should we get him checked out by a doctor?"

"Physically, he looks fine," Rachel said after a moment's pause.

He knew she was already worried about the emotional trauma Joey may have suffered. "You're right, eat first and then pick up my car."

From there, he wasn't sure, other than he wasn't going to take Rachel or Joey back to their home.

Not until he knew for sure they were safe.

Rachel knew she was smothering Joey, but she couldn't seem to stop touching him—his hair, his arm, his knee—to remind herself that he was actually sitting right here beside her.

Thank You, Lord, for keeping my son safe!

There was a tiny voice in the back of her mind telling her that there was a good chance God didn't have anything to do with getting Joey back safely, but she was too emotionally drained to listen. Right now, she found an odd comfort in believing God had been with them through those horrible moments when she'd faced Morales.

"Can we eat at Mr. Burger's?" Joey asked in a soft, hesitant voice. His lack of confidence broke her heart.

"Of course," she agreed, even though she normally avoided those types of fast-food joints like the plague. "Nick, let me know if you see a Mr. Burger's."

"There's one up ahead," Jonah pointed out. She wasn't surprised, as they were everywhere. A few minutes later, they pulled into the parking lot. Jonah swiveled in his seat. "Inside? Or drive-through?"

"Drive-through," Nick said, before she had a chance to respond. "All of us going inside would draw too much attention."

She belatedly remembered his bloodstained jacket. "The drive-through is fine."

Nick warned her to go light on Joey's food, as they placed their order. She went with both a chocolate shake and a soda for her son, along with chicken pieces. No one else ordered anything to eat, including Rachel. The nausea that she'd lived with for the past few hours had dissolved, but she still wasn't hungry.

Jonah kept driving as Joey ate. He only ate about half his food before declaring that he was full. The thought of her son going hungry gnawed away at her, although she was grateful he didn't appear to be physically abused. The only indication of what he'd suffered was the traumatized expression in his eyes.

"That's okay, we can save the rest for later," she said, bundling up the leftovers.

They reached the hotel parking lot where they'd left Nick's car, and there was a heated debate between Jonah and Nick about what to do next.

"Go home to your pregnant wife, Jonah," Nick said stubbornly. "If I need anything more, I'll let you know."

"I'm not leaving when you're wounded," Jonah argued. "Besides, where are you going to go?"

"My mother's uncle has a cabin in Wisconsin," Nick said. "I thought we'd go there for a while. I still have my laptop and we can maybe do some searching while we're there. Hopefully, we'll hear some good news from my boss soon."

"A cabin?" Joey echoed, his eyes wide with enthusiasm. "Can we go to the cabin, Mom? Can we?"

She couldn't bear to deny Joey anything. At least not now. Of course, they'd have to go back home, eventually, to figure out their next steps, now that she didn't have her company anymore. "If that's what Nick thinks is best," she murmured.

"I don't have enough cash to keep going to motels," he said, his tone apologetic. "Besides, Morales is going to report back to whoever hired him that you weren't there alone. I'm worried they might be able to spot my car if we stick around here. I think the cabin is the safest place for us to be right now."

Jonah didn't look convinced. "I still don't like leaving you alone," he grumbled. "But Mallory's due date is next week so I should head home. Promise you'll call if you need me?"

"Yes. And I'll give you the address to my uncle's cabin, too." Nick rattled off the address as Jonah punched it into his phone.

Soon, they were back on the road. Nick had managed to wrap gauze around his arm, which helped stop the bleeding. Jonah insisted on leaving the first-aid kit with them, and Rachel accepted it gratefully, knowing that as soon as they'd reached the cabin, she'd need to do a better job of cleaning up Nick's wound.

She stayed in the backseat with Joey, unwilling to leave him there alone. As Nick's car ate up the miles, crossing over the Illinois/Wisconsin state line, she closed her eyes and clutched her son's hand, wondering if their life would ever be normal again.

Nick glanced in the rearview mirror as he drove, noticing that Rachel had fallen asleep. He was glad she was getting some rest, but Joey, however, was still wide-awake. Dusk was already darkening the sky, and Nick's goal was to make it to the cabin well before nightfall.

"Are you doing okay back there?" he asked softly, trying not to disturb Rachel.

Joey nodded, although his gaze seemed troubled. "The bad man isn't going to come after me again, is he?"

Nick's heart lurched at the panic in Joey's young voice. No matter what happened, the poor kid was going to have nightmares about the kidnapping for a long time to come. He made a mental note to discuss with Rachel the need for Joey to get counseling.

He didn't want to lie to the boy, but he didn't want the child to live in fear, either. He chose his words carefully. "The reason I'm taking you and your mom to the cabin is to keep you safe from the bad man," he said finally. "I've already called my boss and asked him to put out an arrest warrant for the bad man, too. Once he's in jail he won't be able to hurt you or your mom any more."

Joey nodded and seemed to relax at that explanation. "I'm glad you're a police detective," he said.

Nick caught the boy's gaze in the rearview mirror and flashed him a warm smile. "Me, too." He paused, before asking, "Joey, you mentioned you were in a basement room with a mattress, a toilet and a locked door. Do you remember anything else? Anything that might help the police track down the bad man?"

Joey's lower lip trembled as if he might burst out sobbing. And as if she instinctively knew her son was upset, Rachel woke up. "Joey? What's wrong?"

"I c-can't remember anything else," he stuttered. "I couldn't see because the bad man put a black hood over my head!"

Nick winced when Rachel glared at him. "You don't

have to remember anything, sweetie," she said gently, daring Nick to disagree. "I don't want you to worry about the bad man anymore. All that matters is that you're safe here with me. We're going to make sure nothing happens to you, okay?"

"Okay," Joey mumbled.

He sighed and dropped the touchy subject. He didn't want to upset Joey, but at the same time, they needed to know what, if anything, the boy remembered.

Maybe once they reached the cabin, Joey would relax enough to open up about his ordeal. Refusing to discuss what happened wasn't going to help Rachel's son get over what happened.

But talking through the events just might.

He didn't voice his opinion though. Instead, he concentrated on trying to remember the route to his uncle's cabin. The farther north he drove, the more the temperature dropped. There was evidence of a recent light snow, although nothing deep enough to worry about. He hadn't been to Uncle Wally's cabin in the past year, since his uncle had passed away, leaving the cabin to his mother. And since Nick's parents had chosen to retire in Florida last year, he doubted anyone had been up there since he and Wally had been there the summer before his uncle's passing.

Nick's wife and daughter had enjoyed spending time up there, too. He smiled remembering how Sophie had laughed as she played in the fallen leaves. For the first time, remembering his family didn't cause his heart to ache. He'd treasure every moment they had together.

He forced his attention on his surroundings. Twice he had to backtrack, because the area looked so different from what he remembered. But then he caught sight of the red fire sign with the numbers 472 and knew he'd found it. The gravel driveway was barely visible between towering evergreen trees, and so completely overgrown with brush and weeds that he only went far enough to make sure the car was out of sight from the road, before shutting off the engine.

"Sorry, but we'll have to walk in from here," he said, grabbing the bag of clothes in one hand while keeping his weapon ready with the other. Just in case. "I'm afraid we'll get stuck if we drive in any farther."

"That's okay," Rachel replied, opening her door and pushing it against the brush. Joey climbed out right behind her as if eager to be out of the car. He saw Rachel reach for Joey's hand, but when her son eagerly strode through the tall brown grass without so much as glancing at her, she let her hand drop back to her side.

"Be careful," he called to Joey as he came over to walk beside Rachel, their feet crunching against the half-frozen brush.

"I hope there aren't poisonous snakes around here," she said nervously, as she followed her son's progress down the driveway.

"December is too cold for snakes," he assured her. He wanted to reach for her hand but sensed she was still angry with him. "I'm sorry, Rachel. I didn't mean to upset you or Joey."

"Then stop asking him questions about what happened," she said wearily. "Don't you think he's been through enough?"

"I think you've both been through more than enough," Nick said in a low voice. "But we can't afford to relax now. For one thing, Morales knows we saw him and that you didn't come to the barn alone."

"He has the money, what more could he want?" she asked.

"I don't know, but I'm pretty sure he planned to kill you both," he rasped out.

Before Rachel could respond, Joey shouted, "There's the cabin!"

Sure enough, Nick could make out the familiar log cabin through the bare tree branches. The place looked smaller than he remembered, but as long as the wood-burning stove worked, he thought they'd be fine.

"We'll need to discuss this more, later," he said quietly to Rachel. "For now, let's get settled, okay?"

When she nodded, he lengthened his stride to catch up to Joey. Rachel didn't want to believe she and Joey were still in danger, but he knew they were. And he vowed to do whatever it took to keep them safe.

Rachel explored the small kitchen area inside the cabin, relieved to note that there were plenty of canned goods, soups and stew for them to eat. Everything was coated in a thick layer of dust, but nothing was outdated or spoiled. She frowned, knowing that the place needed to be cleaned but that it would be impossible without water.

"First we'll build a fire to make it warm in here," Nick was telling Joey. "Then we're going to prime the pump outside."

"What does that mean?" Joey asked, hovering near Nick as he stacked wood in the large wood-burning stove in the center of the room. There were dried leaves and twigs, too, and soon he had a roaring fire going.

"The well has to be closed up in the winter, or else the pipes will freeze," Nick explained. "We'll prime the pump to get the water running again. I'll show you how it's done."

Rachel watched Joey and Nick interact with a distinct male camaraderie. She knew her son longed for a male role model, which was one of the reasons she'd gotten him involved in sports like basketball. At least his coach was a decent role model for her son.

But to see Joey bond with Nick like this was worrisome. What would happen once this nightmare was over? When Nick went back to his job, leaving her and Joey to make a new life for themselves? She and her son might even have to move in order for her to find work.

The last thing she wanted was for Joey to be hurt again. He'd already suffered so much. The image of the way he'd reacted when Morales ripped the hood off his head was seared into her memory.

Granted, Nick wasn't going to hurt her son on purpose, not the way Morales had. But she knew, with deep certainty, that her son would eventually be hurt just the same.

This was exactly why she hadn't dated or tried to form any relationships with men. And even though she knew most men weren't connected with the Mafia, she wasn't sure she was ready to think about a relationship of any sort. Friendship, yes. But she'd stayed alone because she knew Joey was at a vulnerable and impressionable age. Avoiding relationships was easier than allowing Joey to get close to someone, only to be hurt if the relationship didn't work out. When Nick and Joey went back outside to work on the pump, she grabbed several cans of stew and set them on the counter.

Nick wanted to talk later, and that was just fine with her. Because she wanted to talk to him, too. He had to understand that he needed to keep his distance from Joey.

For her son's sake.

The interior of the cabin warmed up to the point she could take off the bulky jacket and the dark sweatshirt, wearing just the long-sleeved crew neck T-shirt. She stripped off the sheets draping the furniture, sneezing as the dust ticked her nose.

When Nick and Joey returned a few minutes later, they were both grinning from ear to ear. "We did it, Mom!" Joey exclaimed as he and Nick stamped their feet on the mat inside the doorway. "We primed the pump and now we have water."

"Great," she said, forcing a smile when her son looked up at her. "I'm going to clean the place up a bit, and then I thought we'd have the canned beef stew for dinner." Lowering her voice, she slanted a quick glance Nick's way. "Don't forget, we need to change the bandage on your arm, too."

"Plenty of time for that… Let's eat first," Nick said. "We're lucky to have electricity. Apparently my parents are still paying the bills."

"The cabin belongs to your parents?" she asked, curious in spite of herself.

"To my mother," Nick corrected. "I'm going to hike back to the car to get my laptop."

"Can I come, too?" Joey asked.

She opened her mouth to protest but was interrupted by the sound of Nick's phone ringing. He scowled at the display and then walked down the hall, obviously seeking privacy as he answered. "Yeah?"

She couldn't hear much of the conversation and was still trying to figure out a way to prevent Joey from following Nick around like a lost puppy, when Nick came back to the main room, his expression grim.

She tensed, fearing more bad news. "What's wrong?"

"They found the Jeep and, Morales, uh, is no longer a threat," he said carefully, glancing at Joey in a way that told her the man who'd kidnapped her son was dead. "But I'm afraid there's no sign of the duffel bag or the cash."

Her heart squeezed painfully in her chest and she couldn't think of anything to say.

"Unfortunately," Nick continued, "whoever hired Morales appears to have gotten away with it."

TEN

Nick mentally kicked himself as Rachel's expression froze at the news. He felt helpless knowing that Morales had been killed and all of Rachel's money was gone. The chance of finding out who had set up the kidnapping was slim to none at this point, now that their best lead— Morales—had just become, literally, a dead end.

After a long moment, Rachel let out a sigh and shrugged, avoiding his direct gaze. He knew she had to be upset at losing her company like this, but if that was the case, she didn't let on. "I'm glad Morales won't be able to hurt anyone else ever again," she murmured. "Maybe it's wrong, but I can't help thinking he ended up getting exactly what he deserved."

It was on the tip of his tongue to explain how God expected them to forgive those who trespassed against them, but there was a tiny part of him that tended to agree with her. He could forgive Morales and even the guy who'd hired him, but he also knew that those who sinned often paid the price.

If they were alone, he'd go into more detail about the crime scene, but since Joey was listening, he chose his words carefully. "The man behind all this is a professional, but we can't give up. We'll figure out who it is sooner or later."

"I know," she agreed, although her expression didn't exactly radiate confidence.

"Do you want to come for a walk with us to the car?" he offered. Oddly enough, he didn't want to leave her here in the cabin alone, especially after giving her such depressing news. "Shouldn't take us more than fifteen minutes or so."

She hesitated but then nodded. She put both her sweatshirt and the jacket back on and crossed over to join them. He held the door as they trooped outside, and he sniffed, appreciating the woodsy scent intermingled with fireplace smoke that lingered in the air, bringing back fond memories of the good times he'd spent up here with Uncle Wally and with his family.

Joey grabbed a small branch that had fallen from one of the trees and swatted the brush as they walked. Rachel stayed next to Nick, and his hand accidently brushed hers, making him wonder what she would say if he took her hand in his. She'd never said a word about the kiss, although he hadn't mentioned it, either.

But he'd certainly thought about it. Too much. He wanted to kiss her again. But this wasn't the time or the place.

"Are you okay?" he asked under his breath when Joey had gotten far enough ahead of them that he couldn't hear them.

"Fine," she said, kicking a rock with the toe of her athletic shoe. "I knew the risk, right from the start. As I told you before, getting Joey back safe and sound was worth every penny."

Nick couldn't help playing the what-if game. What if he'd insisted on getting the FBI involved? Would they have gotten Joey back and still have Rachel's cash, too? Would they have caught the guy who'd killed Morales? Would Rachel and Joey be safe at home where they belonged?

As much as he wanted Rachel and Joey to be okay, it bothered him to think about the fact that once this was over, he wouldn't be seeing either of them again. Immediately, he felt guilty for even considering replacing Becky and Sophie with Rachel and Joey.

No, he couldn't do it. As much as he cared about Rachel and her son, he and Rachel would be much better off if they simply remained friends once this was over. Maybe he could be sort of a big brother to Joey. Do things like taking him to ball games or just playing catch. Surely, Rachel wouldn't mind having some downtime—being a single mother couldn't be easy.

The more he thought about the possibility of staying in touch with Joey, the more he liked it.

But, first, he had to keep Rachel and Joey safe, while figuring out a way to get her company back.

"I'm going to need your help in order to keep investigating all the possibilities," he murmured.

"I'm not sure how much help I'll be," she protested wearily. "And what's the point of getting your computer? I can't imagine there's any internet available up here."

"The last time I came up with Uncle Wally, I was able to get a signal from someone else's internet tower as they didn't have it secured with a password." He caught her surprised gaze and shrugged. "Figured it was worth a shot to see if the signal is still available."

"There's the car," Joey shouted, running forward as if they were in a race. "Open the trunk, Nick!"

He caught a glimpse of annoyance in Rachel's gaze and tried to figure out what he'd done to upset her as he pushed the button on his key fob, making the truck spring open.

Joey grabbed his computer case and proudly brought it over to him. "Here you go," he announced.

"Thanks, Joey," he said, looping the strap over his shoulder. Before he could say anything more, the boy ran back to shut the trunk for him, too. Nick grabbed the first-aid kit from the front seat and then locked the car.

"We need to talk later," Rachel whispered as Joey made his way back over to where they waited.

"Okay," he agreed, even though deep down he could tell by her tone that, whatever she wanted to talk about, it wasn't going to be good.

Rachel knew she was overreacting to Joey's eagerness to assist Nick, but she couldn't seem to help herself. As they made their way back to the cabin, she quickened her pace to keep up with her son rather than lagging behind with Nick.

"Hey, stop here a minute and look up at the stars," she said to Joey. "Aren't they beautiful?"

"Wow, there's so many," Joey whispered in awe.

"Out here in the country it's easier to see them," she explained. "Back home, the lights from the city tend to get in the way."

Nick came up to stand beside them, tipping his head back to enjoy the view, as well. For a moment, she could almost pretend they were a family, rather than hiding up here fearing for their lives.

This was what Anthony had stolen from her all those years ago. And she hadn't even really understood how much she'd missed what she'd never had, until now.

A loud noise, like a tree branch snapping in two, made her jump, and she instinctively reached out to grab Joey's hand. "Stay with me," she whispered, drawing him close.

"Rachel, take Joey and this stuff back to the cabin," Nick said in a low voice.

A shiver snaked down her spine and she glanced around warily. They were surrounded by trees, which wasn't reassuring, since she couldn't see much in the darkness. She took the computer case from him and slung it over her shoulder. She held the first-aid kit tight to her chest. Despite being irked with Nick earlier, she was loath to leave him now. "Come with us," she urged softly.

"Could be nothing more than a deer or some other animal," he assured her. "Go inside and lock the door. I'm going to take a look around."

Nick was armed and could probably take care of himself, yet it was still difficult to leave him alone. But now that she had her son back, she wasn't about to risk losing him again, so she gave a jerky nod.

"Come on, Joey," she whispered, shielding him as best as she could as they quickly ran in the direction of the cabin. Even after getting safely inside, she couldn't relax. She secured the dead bolt lock into place, set down the laptop and the first-aid kit on the rough-hewn kitchen table and then doused the lights. She hoped the darkness would shield them from anyone watching from outside, although there wasn't much she could do about the yellow glow of the fire.

"I thought the bad man was gone?" Joey asked fearfully.

"He is gone," she said, trying to smile. "You heard what Nick said—I'm sure the noise was probably from a deer. Nick is being extra careful because he's a police detective and that's what policemen do. Come sit on the sofa in front of the fire with me."

Joey went over to the sofa and she desperately searched for something to use as a weapon. A kitchen knife would only work if the thug came in close, so she bypassed that option. Her gaze fell on the trio of fireplace instruments Nick had used earlier to help start the fire. The poker was long, made of cast iron and was pointy on the end. Since the poker gave her the best chance to protect herself and Joey, she carried the stand of fireplace instruments to the right side of the sofa and set the poker so that it was well within reach, before she snuggled in next to her son.

"I'm scared," Joey whimpered beside her.

Her heart squeezed in her chest. "I'm not going to let anything happen to you, sweetie, and neither will Nick," she said. "You're not alone anymore. We're safe here inside the cabin with Nick protecting us."

He responded by burying his face against her arm, clinging tight. She hugged him close, a wave of helpless despair washing over her. How much more could the poor kid take? He'd already been through so much. More than any child should have to bear.

She'd thought that getting Joey back would solve all her problems, but she was wrong. Because they were here, cowering in the darkness of the cabin, fearing the worst.

Nick was right—they needed to keep investigating in order to find the person who'd set up the kidnapping. Because they wouldn't be safe until they knew the truth.

Tense with fear and worry, she stared at the front door of the cabin, hoping and praying Nick would return soon.

Nick melted into the trees, moving slowly and carefully, the way Uncle Wally had taught him all those years ago. He hadn't liked hunting deer the way Uncle Wally had, but he'd learned enough from his uncle to move quietly through the woods. He held his gun ready, in case he stumbled across a man or wild beast.

White-tailed deer tended to feed in the early morning

or early evening, so there was a good possibility that a buck or a doe moving through the woods had made the noise. There weren't bears in the area, at least not that he knew about. The snapped branch had seemed too loud for a small animal like a raccoon or a skunk, although possums could grow to a fairly good size. Maybe one had fallen out of a tree?

Nick was sure he hadn't been followed on the ride up to the cabin, so he found it hard to believe the kidnapper could have found them. Even if the kidnapper had the brains and the means to track him here, it would take a lot of expert digging to connect the cabin to him.

He made a slow, wide circle around the cabin. He didn't see anything out of the ordinary, no signs of anyone lurking around. He came across a deer bed about twenty yards behind the cabin, which made him relax. Deer were close by, so it was likely that's what they'd heard.

There was a small structure back there, too, and he moved forward cautiously. When he got closer, he wrinkled his nose at the smell, realizing this was the old outhouse that Uncle Wally had used before installing the well and the small but functional bathroom. He opened the door and flashed his small penlight inside, to make sure it was indeed empty. Then he made his way back around to the front of the cabin.

The lights were off inside, although he could see the flickering flames from the fireplace. He stood on the porch for another few minutes, straining to listen. When he didn't hear anything, he tapped lightly on the door. "Rachel? Open up, it's me, Nick."

After a few minutes, he heard her disengage the lock and open the door. "Did you find anything?" she asked.

"Just a deer bed in back of the cabin," he said cheerfully. He closed the door and relocked it. "Not only does that prove that deer are close by, but also that they've felt safe enough to make a bed here."

Rachel's smile was strained as she nodded and glanced over at her son, who was burrowed into a corner of the sofa. "Did you hear that, Joey? There's a deer bed behind the cabin."

"What kind of bed?" Joey asked, a puzzled frown furrowing his brow.

"Deer like to sleep in tall grass. Not only is the grass soft, but it also keeps the deer hidden during the day. In the early-evening hours they get up and move through the trees, looking for something to eat."

"What do they eat?" Joey asked.

"Speaking of eating, how about I heat up our supper?" Rachel suggested, heading over to the kitchen area.

He crossed over to sit beside Joey. "White-tailed deer are vegetarian, meaning they eat grass, leaves and berries. In the winter, when there aren't as many leaves, they eat the bark off the trees." He remembered his uncle Wally explaining that culling the herd of deer by hunting them in season was better than letting them starve to death. Logically he agreed, but that didn't make it any easier to kill the beautiful, graceful animals.

Joey continued to ask questions and he patiently answered them, figuring that the more they talked, the more the child would be able to relax and feel safe.

"Dinner's ready," Rachel called a few minutes later. Joey crawled out from his spot on the sofa to cross over to the kitchen table. Nick threw another log on the fire and then joined them.

He clasped his hands together and bowed his head. "Heavenly Father, we thank You for providing us food and shelter tonight, and we ask that You continue to watch over us, keeping us safe from harm. Amen."

"Amen," Rachel echoed.

After a brief moment, Joey, too, said, "Amen."

Nick lifted his head and smiled at them both. "Thanks for praying with me. And this looks great, Rachel, I appreciate you cooking dinner."

"All I did was heat up the beef stew in a pot on the electric burner," she protested. "I don't think that counts as cooking."

"It does in my book," he said. The hearty beef stew hit the spot and Rachel and Joey must have been hungry too, because between the three of them, they finished every bite.

"I'll clean up," he said, carrying his and Joey's empty bowls over to the sink.

Rachel looked as if she might protest but then must have decided to take the opportunity to spend time with her son. He heard them exploring the cabin, although since it wasn't very big, it didn't take them long. Rachel brought a quilt with her from the back bedroom and covered them with it as they sat on the sofa, staring into the fire.

Seeing Rachel snuggled up next to Joey filled him with bittersweet longing. If he were alone, he'd probably think about Becky, but right now, he found himself captivated by the way the light from the fire flickered over Rachel's hair.

Washing the dishes didn't take long, and when he finished he pulled out the computer and tried to find the wireless signal that he'd used the last time he was here. Sure enough, the signal was weak but available, as it still wasn't password protected.

He searched for information on Dr. Karl Errol since he still thought that Josie Gardner's suicide wasn't just a coincidence. He soon discovered that Dr. Karl Errol had attended Johns Hopkins to earn his doctorate and had worked for a large international pharmaceutical company before coming to work for Rachel.

Sitting back in the chair, he tried to figure out why a highly respected research scientist from Johns Hopkins had left a large pharmaceutical corporation to work for Simon Inc.

"Joey's asleep," Rachel said, interrupting his thoughts. She came over to the table, pulled up a chair next to him and sat down. "You should let me take a look at your arm."

Nick grimaced and then nodded reluctantly. He worked his arm out of the sweatshirt sleeve while she jumped up and heated up water on the two-burner stove.

The angle was too awkward for him to see the extent of the injury and he was glad it didn't throb as much as it had at first. Rachel came over with the first-aid kit they'd brought in from the car, along with a small pan of hot water.

"This might hurt," she warned as she picked up a soft cloth and began cleaning the wound.

He didn't say anything, too distracted by her nearness as she fussed over him. He couldn't help remembering the kiss they'd shared and wondered if she'd let him kiss her again. Soon.

"Almost finished," she murmured, and he blinked, realizing she was putting antibiotic ointment over the flesh wound before wrapping it with gauze.

"Thanks," he murmured huskily. When she turned away to take the water back over to the sink, he carefully put his arm back into the sleeve of his sweatshirt.

Once she'd finished cleaning everything up, she came back to the table. It took all his willpower to turn his attention to the investigation at hand. "Tell me about Dr. Karl Errol. How long has he worked for you?"

Rachel frowned. "He's been working for me for about three years now," she said slowly.

"How did you come to hire him? Did he apply for a job? Or did you purposefully recruit him away from his other company?"

"Neither. Josie Gardner is actually the one who recommended him for the job. She apparently met him at a research convention and talked about some of the work we were doing. He was very interested and Josie convinced me to make him an offer. To be honest, I was surprised when he actually accepted it."

"Why do you think he did? Accept the job, I mean?"

Rachel shrugged. "During our interview, he mentioned that he liked the way I put so much time and effort into research and development for new medications. He claimed that his old company had gone stagnant and that he was looking for change."

Nick hesitated, knowing that she wasn't going to like his next question. "Could it be that he was searching for a place where no one was constantly looking over his shoulder? Because maybe he liked to cut corners? What if the problem with your new diabetes medication happened in the first place because he hid something important?"

"No way… Josie would have been all over that," she said.

"Maybe that's why she committed suicide."

She stared at him for a long moment. "It's possible, but why would Karl do something like that in the first place? Why bring forward a medication that has life-threatening side effects?" She blew out a breath. "Don't you see? There's no logical reason why anyone, especially a well-respected researcher, would risk ruining their reputation and their career by doing something so crazy."

He hated to admit she had a point. What could the

motivation be? He shifted several scenarios through his mind. "What if he's doing it on purpose to sabotage your company?" he mused.

Rachel closed her eyes and rubbed them. "Again, Nick, for what purpose? What's the link between this and Joey's kidnapping? I keep telling you that none of this makes any sense. The only logical explanation is that someone within the Mafia needed cash and orchestrated Joey's kidnapping to get it." She sighed impatiently. "Sabotaging the company would only make it more difficult to come up with the money. Whatever is going on within the company probably isn't connected."

He understood why she chose to believe the Mafia was behind the kidnapping. For one thing, the threatening letters did seem to point to the crime syndicate. But what if someone inside her company had sent them, pretending to be with the Mafia? He thought she had blinders on when it came to thinking anything bad about the people who worked for her.

"Rachel, hear me out for a minute, okay?" he said, leaning in toward her. "You said the lawsuit was filed last year and that you have already offered a generous settlement, right?"

"Yes, that's correct."

"Was your settlement accepted?"

She flushed and shook her head. "Not yet."

Interesting. "What if that was essentially the start of this mess? What if all of this—the failed medication, the lawsuit and now the kidnapping were just ways to put you out of business?"

"Who would want to put me out of business?"

"You tell me," he countered. "Which company is your biggest competition?"

"Global Pharmaceuticals," she answered automatically.

ELEVEN

Rachel didn't want to believe Nick's theory, but she couldn't deny that his idea had merit. "Seems odd that Global would go to such drastic lengths to put me under," she said softly. "But, okay, let's say they did convince Karl to sabotage my company. And that the failed diabetes medication was part of the master plan. How does kidnapping Joey fit into the picture? Removing me as the CEO isn't going to put the company under. Gerry Ashton has been working for the company over the past seventeen years and he's perfectly capable of running the company without me."

"Isn't there anything about your management styles that could make the difference between success and failure?" Nick pressed.

Rachel clenched her teeth in frustration. She didn't understand why he remained so focused on someone working against her from inside the company rather than the Mafia link.

Although now that Morales was dead, she was forced to admit they might never know for sure who was behind the kidnapping.

"The only difference between Gerry and me is that I

Global Pharmaceuticals. The same company where Karl Errol used to work. "That's it! The link we've been looking for. Don't you think it's possible that Karl Errol, who used to work for Global Pharmaceuticals, is actually doing corporate espionage for them? That he's sabotaging your company on purpose?"

The dawning horror in her eyes made him feel bad for shattering her trust, but, at the same time, he firmly believed they were finally onto something.

Now, all he needed was a way to prove it.

take more risks in research and development," she said. "Gerry tends to be more conservative."

"That's all? Nothing else?" Nick appeared disappointed by her response.

"The only other thing we disagreed about was settling the lawsuit," she admitted. She still remembered the heated argument they'd had. Gerry had pushed so hard she had been forced to take the issue to the board of directors. "He wanted to continue to fight, but I managed to convince the board that settling right away would be better for us in the long run. And there's still hope that the lawsuit will be settled soon."

"How long has Ashton worked for you?" he probed.

"I've only been in charge as the CEO for the past three years, since my father died. Gerry was a VP colleague during the years my father was in charge." Before he could ask another question, she quickly changed the subject. "I need to talk to you about Joey."

Nick's eyebrows lifted. "What about him?"

She took a deep breath and released it slowly, trying to figure out a way to articulate her concern without hurting his feelings. "Joey is at a vulnerable age, and I think it's clear he's looking for a father figure. I've noticed he's been following you around, and I'd appreciate it if you didn't encourage him. Please try to keep your distance."

He stared at her for a long moment. "I haven't encouraged him on purpose," he finally said. "Besides, I'm not sure I understand what your problem is. Showing your son how to build a fire and how to prime a well isn't a big deal."

"Maybe not, but can't you see that I don't want him to rely on you too much? Once this is over…" She trailed off, unable or maybe unwilling to put her deepest fears into words. "I just don't want him hurt," she repeated lamely.

"I'm sorry you feel that way, Rachel," Nick said with a frown. "I was hoping that Joey and I could hang out once in a while, even after this is over."

Her jaw dropped in surprise. It had never occurred to her that Nick would want to continue to see her son. And, for some reason, she found the idea disconcerting. "Well, uh, I guess I'll think about it," she said, unable to come up with a good reason for refusing him outright.

Nick's intense gaze bored into hers and she squirmed in her seat, feeling as if he was seeing right through her. She couldn't explain why the two of them forging a relationship after this was over bothered her so much, but it did. She glanced at her sleeping son and rose to her feet. "I'm going to take Joey to the back bedroom."

"Good idea," Nick agreed readily. "I'll stay out here, since I'll need to keep feeding wood into the fireplace, anyway."

She nodded, relieved to have an excuse to avoid Nick for the rest of the night. The way she'd warned Nick to stay away from her son was just as important for her to remember, as well. In all honesty, she was becoming far too dependent on Nick. She crossed over to lift her sleeping son into her arms. At nine years old, he was too big to carry, but she managed, staggering under his weight yet unwilling to ask Nick for help.

The bedroom was cool, being farther away from the fire. She set Joey on the bed and, amazingly, he didn't wake up. She shivered and searched for more blankets. Luckily, she'd found earlier a huge hope chest filled with handmade quilts. She retrieved several of them to use as covers and then stretched out on the bed next to Joey.

After everything they'd been through, she was physically exhausted. But her mind raced, replaying every moment of the past twenty-four hours. No matter what she tried, her mind wouldn't settle and it was only after she recited the Lord's Prayer, the only prayer she remembered from her childhood, that she finally managed to fall asleep.

Nick dozed, waking himself up every few hours to put more wood on the fire and to make sure everything was all right outside. He hadn't gotten much sleep the night before, when they'd spent the night in the car, so he had to depend on the deeply ingrained training his four years in the Marine Corps had given him in order to keep watch, despite his bone-deep exhaustion.

He tried to formulate a plan for the following day, but every time he closed his eyes, he fell asleep. When he dragged himself off the sofa at six in the morning, dawn had lightened the darkness and the fire had dwindled.

It didn't take long to bring the glowing embers back to life. Since it was too late to go back to sleep, he washed up in the small bathroom. He opened the medicine cabinet, thankful to find a somewhat rusty razor along with some ancient shaving cream. There were other items his uncle had left up there, too, but he limited himself to using the razor.

When he came out of the bathroom, he heard movement from the back bedroom. He wasn't surprised when Joey's head peeked out from behind the door. "Hi, Nick," he whispered.

"Good morning, Joey," he whispered back. Rachel must still be sleeping or he was sure she'd have already put an end to the brief conversation. At some point during the wee hours of the morning, he'd figured out that the main reason Rachel didn't want him spending time with her son was that she thought he might get too attached to Joey, after the way he'd lost his own child.

Still, he couldn't ignore the kid gazing at him with wide green eyes, so he gestured for Joey to come out of the bedroom. "Are you hungry?" he asked.

Joey nodded eagerly and slipped through the narrow opening, quietly closing the door behind him. The boy was wearing the same clothes as the day before, not that he seemed to mind. "What's for breakfast?"

Good question. "I don't know. Let's take a look, okay?" He put a hand behind Joey's back, urging him down the short hall to the main room. Rachel couldn't be too upset with him for not waking her up, he rationalized, since she obviously needed the rest. "I think I saw some oatmeal," he said to Joey. "Do you like oatmeal?"

"With brown sugar," the boy said excitedly.

"I'm not sure we have any brown sugar," he said cautiously. "But I think there's some regular sugar, which should work just as well."

Joey stopped in front of the fire, holding his hands toward the flames as if he were cold. "Did you keep the fire going all night, Nick?"

"Yep. It's our main source of heat for the cabin." He found a box of oatmeal, but it wasn't the instant kind, so he followed the cooking directions on the label.

Joey kept up a constant stream of chatter, and Nick couldn't help admiring the boy's quick mind. Rachel's son was interested in everything, from camping to sports. To help pass the time until breakfast was ready, he showed Joey how to carve small animals in pieces of wood with his penknife.

As they talked, he realized he couldn't have kept his distance from the boy if his life depended on it.

When the oatmeal was ready, he poured the steaming breakfast into two medium-size bowls. His uncle actually did have some brown sugar stored in an airtight container, so he liberally sprinkled their breakfast before taking Joey's hand in his.

"We have to pray before we eat," he said.

"Why?" Joey asked, his gaze curious.

Nick sensed he was heading down a path Rachel might not approve, but he wanted Joey to be given the option of believing in God. "Because we need to thank God for the food we're about to eat."

Joey pursed his lips. "Is God in heaven?" he asked.

"Yes, and He's always there for us, whenever we need Him."

Joey frowned for a moment. "You think God was with me when I was in the dark, stinky room?" he asked.

Nick's heart clenched and he nodded. "Yes, Joey, I do. Your mom and I were praying for God to watch over you the whole time you were gone."

"Really?" Joey brightened at the news. "I wish I would have known that," he confessed. "Maybe I wouldn't have been so scared."

Nick wished the same thing, but no sense in going back, trying to change the past. In his opinion, it was never too late to believe in the Lord.

He closed his eyes and bowed his head. "Heavenly Father, we thank You for the food and shelter You've provided for us, and we ask You again, to keep us safe from harm. Amen."

"Amen," Joey echoed.

Nick lifted his head and opened his eyes to find Rachel standing behind Joey's chair. She'd approached so quietly he hadn't heard her. He tensed, expecting an argument, but she simply added "Amen" to his prayer.

He immediately pushed back from the table. "Here, take my bowl of oatmeal, I'll get more."

She hesitated for a moment but then accepted his hot

cereal and took a seat next to her son. He was touched at how they both waited until he returned before eating.

They were too busy eating to talk much. He watched with amusement as Joey quickly emptied his bowl. "Can I have seconds?" he asked anxiously.

"Of course," Nick responded, exchanging a knowing look with Rachel. Joey hadn't eaten much yesterday, but it appeared his appetite had returned.

"So what's the plan for today?" Rachel asked.

"I'm not sure yet," he answered honestly. "I should check in with my boss again, see if he can give us anything further to go on."

She darted a glance at Joey and nodded. He sensed there was more she wanted to say but didn't feel she could talk freely in front of Joey.

When they were finished with breakfast, Rachel insisted on doing the dishes, so he took the opportunity to do a quick perimeter check. The only problem was that Joey wanted to come with him.

He glanced helplessly over at Rachel, silently pleading with her to help. As much as he liked spending time with the boy, he needed to make sure the area around the cabin was secure. And he didn't want Joey to come outside with him until he was convinced they were safe.

"Joey, I need you to dry the dishes for me, okay? There will be time later for you to play outside."

"That's women's work," Joey mumbled, lightly kicking at the chair.

"No, it's not," Nick corrected. "I did the dishes last night, so it's only fair you take your turn."

Joey's disgruntled expression faded as he considered Nick's words. "All right," he finally agreed, going over to pick up the dish towel.

Rachel ruefully rolled her eyes and he quickly ducked

outside before he broke into a wide smile. Sometimes, it paid to be able to double-team kids.

The thought caused him to pause before heading sound-lessly into the dense wood. As a single mother, Rachel didn't have anyone to count on when it came to raising Joey. She had to play the role of both parents.

Was it any wonder she was so protective?

He focused on the task at hand, moving slowly and methodically so he didn't miss any signs now that it was daylight. The day was overcast, denying him the sun-light he would have preferred. He stood in the clearing, imagining that the log cabin was the center of a large clock with the south side, straight ahead from the door, at the twelve-o'clock position. He began to make his way around the circle.

In the three-o'clock area, he found a tuft of brown fab-ric stuck to the tip of a branch that was roughly shoulder height. He stared at it for a long minute, trying to estimate how long it had been there.

He could check the internet for how long it had been since the last snowfall, but he figured, from the dusting on the ground, that it had been within the past day or two. But if the snowfall had been light, the tuft of fabric might have survived intact.

By December the gun deer-hunting season was over, but bow-hunting season lasted until January. Was it pos-sible that someone dressed in camouflage-colored cloth-ing had been through here recently, bow hunting? Uncle Wally's land was posted, but considering no one had been up here lately, he figured the No Trespassing signs didn't mean much.

He wanted to believe there was a hunter in the woods rather than some other random person. Because if it wasn't a hunter, then he was forced to consider the fact that this cabin might not be as safe as he'd thought.

Rachel finished the dishes and then went over to straighten up the quilts on the bed. Near the end table, she found an old Bible. Opening the flap, she was surprised to discover it belonged to Nick's mother.

She carried the Bible back to the main living area, wondering if Nick's mother had left it here or if it belonged to Nick, himself? The book was clearly old and well used. The edges of the paper were gold and there were small cutouts for each of the Bible sections. In the center there was a place for family names and she discovered it had been filled in with neat handwriting stating the names of Nick and his two sisters.

She hadn't known about Nick's sisters. And she realized there were probably a lot of things she didn't know about Nick.

Curious, she opened the book and scanned the various chapters. It wasn't easy to decipher the meaning of the writing since, according to the title page, it was written in the Authorized King James Version.

"What are you reading?" Joey asked, coming over to sit next to her on the sofa.

She glanced down at her son, remembering the conversation he'd had with Nick before breakfast. It had nearly broken her heart to hear Joey describe how alone he'd felt in the dark room where Morales had kept him. She realized now that she'd done her son a disservice by not teaching him religion. "This is a Bible, which is a collection of God's words," she explained, hoping she was describing it right.

"Are there stories in there?" he queried, leaning over to see for himself.

"Yes, there are," she replied, although she wasn't sure exactly where they were. She vaguely remembered some Bible stories from her childhood, but how to find them in this huge book?

She opened the Bible to the New Testament, and the pages opened to the Gospel according to Saint John. "'In the beginning was the Word and the Word was with God and the Word was God,'" she read out loud. Joey leaned against her, seemingly content so she continued, "'The same was in the beginning with God. All things were made by him and without him was not any thing made that was made. In him was life; and the life was the light of men.'"

Soon, she got into the rhythm of the words, and the lyrical quality of the text helped her to relax. So intent was she on reading that she didn't hear Nick return.

When she glanced up, she saw him watching her, a gentle smile on his face. She stumbled over the next sentence and then stopped.

"You sound like you've been reading the Bible your entire life," he murmured, admiration reflected in his gaze.

She felt herself blush. "I hope it's okay that I'm reading your mother's Bible," she said. "I found it on the bedside table in our room."

"She'd be thrilled," he assured her. "John's Gospel is one of my favorites. Although you also might try the book of Psalms—those are where I go when I need to reconnect with God. Or we might want to review the Gospel surrounding the birth of Jesus, as that's what Christmas is all about."

"All right," she agreed, thinking that this was the first time in her entire life that she'd had a conversation about the Bible with a man.

Actually, with anyone. Yet she found it wasn't the least bit awkward, at least with Nick.

Joey scrambled off the sofa and ran over to Nick. "Did you find any deer in the deer bed?" he asked, the Bible stories forgotten.

"Nope, didn't see any deer there today," he said with a wry smile.

She frowned and set the Bible aside. "What did you find?" she asked, sensing there was something bothering him.

He shrugged. "Could be nothing, but I think I'll call Jonah, just in case."

She did not like the sound of that. "Just in case what?"

He hesitated. "Just in case the bit of fabric I found outside doesn't belong to a hunter poaching on my uncle's land."

Nick tried Jonah several times before he connected with his friend. "I might need some backup," he said bluntly.

"What happened?" Jonah asked.

In the background he could hear Mallory's voice but not exactly what she was saying. "I found some fabric stuck to a tree branch about fifty feet from the cabin. Can't be sure it's a random hunter or someone who could have followed us."

There was a moment of silence. "I want to help you, Nick, but Mallory has been having contractions. She says it's probably false labor, since she's not due until next week, but I'm not willing to take the chance."

"Hey, no problem," he hastened to assure his friend. "Stay with Mallory, I'm sure we'll be fine."

"Maybe you should call for backup? Or, find another place to stay," Jonah suggested.

"Yeah, maybe." Neither option thrilled him. He trusted his boss but didn't want to bring in anyone new. And if they left, he'd have to use his credit card, since he was almost out of cash. If the Mafia was involved, they likely had the ability to track them that way. Not to mention, he rather liked the coziness of the cabin. "Take care of Mallory, and call me if I'm going to be an honorary uncle."

"Nick, wait," Jonah said, before he could hang up. "I did find something interesting. I know you weren't keen on the Mafia angle, but guess who's back in Chicago?"

Nick rubbed his hand along the back of his neck. "Tell me you didn't find Frankie Caruso."

"Bing, bing, bing—you win the grand prize," Jonah joked.

Nick could barely drudge up a smile. "Where was he spotted?"

"That's what was so interesting. He was at a fundraiser put together by the mayor to raise money for diabetes research."

Diabetes research? "Are you sure?"

"I'm sure, but check it out online if you need more information."

Another coincidence. "Why does the Chicago mayor care about diabetes?"

"Because his wife was recently diagnosed with diabetes, and he thinks there should be more research into finding a cure."

"Okay, thanks for the heads-up," Nick said. After ending the call, he crossed over to the table and booted up the laptop.

He quickly pulled up a search engine and put in Caruso's name along with the word *fund-raiser*. Sure enough, there he was standing next to the mayor and his wife.

As he stared at the elder Caruso, he couldn't help thinking that Rachel may have been right all along. Caruso might have been the mastermind behind Joey's kidnapping. Seeing as he was such good friends with the mayor, it could be that Caruso wasn't happy about Rachel's failed diabetes medication. Could be that the mayor had a bone to pick with Rachel's company, too.

What better revenge than to kidnap her son, forcing her to sell off her shares of the company? And the added bonus? Making himself rich in the process.

TWELVE

Rachel could tell something was bothering Nick, but with Joey sitting right there, she was hesitant to ask too many questions about the investigation.

"Mom, can I work on my deer carving?" Joey asked from his favorite spot on the sofa.

"Deer carving?" she echoed with a raised brow. Nick's sheepish expression gave him away. "You taught him to do that?" she asked.

"Um, yeah. Hope you don't mind."

She should mind, but oddly she was touched that he'd taken the time. "Are you sure it's safe?"

"My uncle taught me how to carve when I was about his age, and I stressed the importance of being careful with the knife."

"All right, go ahead, Joey." At least carving would help keep her son occupied. She crossed the room to glance over Nick's shoulder at the computer screen. Only to be distracted by the scent of his shaving cream. It was strangely comforting and she had to fight not to put her arms around him.

Nick seemed impervious to her quandary. "Do you recognize anyone in the photograph?" he asked.

Forcing herself to concentrate, she narrowed her gaze

on the photo. Suddenly, her stomach clenched with recognition. She pointed at the screen. "Frankie Caruso."

"Yeah, with the Chicago mayor and his wife," Nick murmured. "The mayor's wife was recently diagnosed with diabetes, and this was a fund-raiser to support research for a cure."

Another link to diabetes. "I'm sure Frankie is the one who hired Morales," she said. "It's the only thing that makes sense."

"Maybe." Nick jammed his fingers through his hair. "I need to go through the entire timeline from start to finish. There has to be something we're missing."

"I'll help," she offered. Her phone rang and she pulled it out of her sweatshirt pocket, surprised to see there was still one bar of battery left. Wincing, she saw the caller was Edith. It seemed like days since she'd spoken to her assistant. "Hi, Edith, how are you?"

"I'm putting in my notice," the woman said in a crisp tone. "You should have told me that you intended to sell off your shares of the company, Rachel. If I'd have known, I would have looked for somewhere else to work."

The reproach in the older woman's tone only sharpened her guilt. "I'm sorry, Edith, you're right—I should have told you. But why are you leaving? I'm sure Gerry could use all the support he can get."

"Gerry Ashton is not you, Rachel. Nor is he your father. I've been loyal to the both of you, but now that you're both gone, I see no need to stay on."

She was flabbergasted with Edith's decision. "Maybe you should take some time to reconsider," she said. "Gerry has been with the company for seventeen years—I'm sure everything will be fine."

"I've made my decision." Edith's tone held an underlying note of steel. "And I'm telling you because you're the one I was working for."

Rachel sensed there was nothing she could say to talk her senior assistant out of resigning. "I'll make sure you get all your vacation pay, Edith," she said, even though technically she didn't own the company anymore. Surely the payroll staff would still listen to her. "And if you change your mind—"

"I won't. Goodbye, Rachel."

Rachel disconnected from the call just as her phone battery gave out.

"Edith resigned?" Nick asked with a dark frown.

"Apparently." She sank into the seat next to Nick, trying to grapple with the news. "I feel terrible about this. Edith has been with the company for thirty years."

"It's not as if you sold off your shares on purpose," Nick reminded her gently. "This isn't your fault."

Yes, it was her fault, but she couldn't deny that she'd do it all again in a heartbeat if it meant getting Joey back safely. Up until now, she'd convinced herself that her life was the only one impacted by her decision.

She took a deep breath and met Nick's sympathetic gaze. There was nothing she could do now but move forward. "Let's work on that timeline…."

Nick wanted nothing more than to reach over and pull Rachel close, to comfort her. She looked as if she'd lost her best friend, and maybe she had. He suspected Edith had been her rock, especially after her father passed away.

There wasn't anything he could say to her to make her feel better, so he took her cue and agreed to work on the timeline.

"I need paper," he muttered. He'd prefer a large whiteboard or bulletin board, but paper would do in a pinch, far better than the computer.

"I think there was some in the bedroom, I'll be right back." Rachel returned a few minutes later with a tattered notebook. "Sorry, but this is all I could find," she said.

"Perfect," he said, taking the notebook from her hands. Their fingers brushed and he tried to ignore the tingling that radiated up his arm. This wasn't the time or the place to think about kissing Rachel again. He tore several sheets of paper out and set them side by side.

"We should probably start with the failed diabetes medication," Rachel said.

He nodded in agreement. "Do you remember the dates and times of the letters and phone calls?"

She reached over and took the pencil from his hand to write in the information. Her nearness was disconcerting. "And here's the date I called you," she added.

"And the same day, you took Joey to his basketball game," he said.

"Yes, that's the part that has bothered me." She scowled at the timeline. "I don't think I was followed, for sure not by the black truck."

Nick had to concur, since he'd followed her and had made sure no one had followed him. "It seemed the kidnappers were one step ahead of us for the first twenty-four hours—until we exchanged your cell phone."

"You thought they were tracking the GPS in my phone, right?"

"Was it a company phone?" he asked, slanting a sideways glance at her. "Or your personal phone?"

"It was a company phone, which also served my personal needs. I saw no reason to have two phones, and it's handy to have ready access to my work email at all times."

"Okay, so who would have access to the serial number for your company phone?" he asked.

Rachel shrugged. "Lots of people. Edith, for sure, and probably some of the staff in billing."

"Do you have an informatics department? Who takes care of interfacing your work email to your phone?"

"We contract with a small company, called Tech Support Inc., and they come in once a month for a day or two to update the computers, scan for problems, that kind of thing."

He'd never heard of Tech Support Inc. but a quick internet search didn't reveal anything alarming. "How long have you had a contract with them?"

"For several years," Rachel responded. "I hardly think they would give out private information like that."

"They might to someone within your company," Nick countered. "Say for instance, Karl Errol?"

"Maybe, but I doubt it. Karl is a researcher—wouldn't they see that as suspicious?"

"Not if he gave them a good reason. Or if he had someone else call, pretending to be you or Edith." He stared at the timeline for a moment. "I think it's clear that whoever tracked your cell phone was someone from inside your company, Rachel," he said slowly. "Not Frankie Caruso."

Rachel's emotions rolled up and down like a yo-yo, and Nick wasn't helping matters. First Frankie was involved, and then he wasn't. The kidnapping was related to her failed diabetes medication, and then it wasn't.

Her head ached and she pressed her fingertips to her temples, trying to ease the pressure. "I'm not sure what to think," she said finally. "Maybe we should go back to Chicago, see if we can talk to Karl."

Nick was still entering dates and times into their makeshift chart. "Josie's suicide is bothering me," he muttered half to himself. "Would make more sense if it was actually murder staged to look like a suicide."

That caught her attention. "Why?"

"Because suicide indicates she felt guilty about something," he explained. "If she was part of the cover-up related to the failed diabetes medication, then okay, I could buy that idea. But if she stumbled onto the truth and intended to come talk to you about it, then I'm more inclined to believe it was murder."

A chill snaked down Rachel's spine. "The meeting I was supposed to have with Karl and Josie the day I received the threatening letter and called you—it was set up by Josie. She told me that she had something important to discuss with me and insisted that Karl be there, too."

"That fits with my homicide theory," he said. "Do you think Edith knows anything more about what Josie wanted to discuss with you?"

"I doubt it. Edith was more concerned with fitting all the necessary meetings into my schedule. She wouldn't ask Josie why she wanted to talk to me. If Josie said it was important, then she'd find the time to make it happen."

Nick grimaced and then turned his attention back to the timeline. She found it hard to concentrate, though, too preoccupied by the idea of her employee possibly being murdered.

How Nick worked homicide cases on a regular basis was beyond her comprehension. She admired his strength and his dedication, more than she should.

She glanced over to the sofa and frowned when she didn't see her son sitting there. For a moment panic set in. "Where's Joey?"

Nick glanced up in surprise. "He was there a few minutes ago."

She jumped up from her seat next to Nick. "Joey?" she called, her tone sharper than she intended.

Joey didn't answer but suddenly there was a loud crash from the direction of the bathroom. Without hesitation, she rushed over. "Joey?" She knocked on the bathroom door. "Are you okay in there?"

"The smell," she heard Joey whimper. Concerned, she opened the door, grateful there was no lock.

Joey was huddled on the floor, silent tears streaming down his cheeks. The medicine cabinet door was open and it took a minute for the harsh scent of aftershave to register, because she was focused on the smears of blood on the sink. "Joey, what happened?"

"Don't tell Nick," he whimpered.

She tried to figure out what happened. "Don't tell Nick what?"

"I cut myself with the knife," Joey managed to blurt out between sobs. "I didn't want to tell you because I didn't want Nick to be disappointed in me."

Her heart wrenched in her chest, and she knelt beside Joey and pulled him into her arms. "Nick won't be disappointed in you, sweetie. Let me see the cut."

He held out his hand, and she could see the slim cut along the pad of his thumb. There was a small bit of blood and she needed to examine the cut to make sure it wasn't so deep it needed stitches.

"Let's get that cleaned up, okay?" she suggested calmly.

"I don't like the smell," Joey said again.

She frowned and turned on the faucet, sticking his thumb beneath the gently running water. The broken bottle of stinky aftershave was lying on the floor, the liquid seeping into the wooden floor. "What happened, Joey?"

"I was looking for a Band-Aid," he said, sniffling back his tears. "And I accidently knocked it over."

"Is everything okay?" Nick asked from the doorway.

Joey's big green eyes once again filled with tears. "I'm sorry, Nick."

"Hey now, don't cry." Nick sent her a pleading look. "I don't care about that bottle of aftershave, it was old anyway."

But Joey shook his head. "No, I'm sorry about the knife," he said. "I was being careful like you said, but it slipped and I didn't want you to know I cut myself."

"I'm not mad at you, Joey, so don't worry about it, okay?" Nick flashed her son a reassuring smile.

Rachel was glad to see that the cut wasn't that deep, and she held Joey's hand under the warm water as she rummaged in the open medicine cabinet. "Do you have any tape and gauze I can use to keep it clean and dry?" she asked.

"We still have Jonah's first-aid kit in the kitchen," Nick assured her. She relaxed and nodded, remembering how she'd used it to change the dressing on Nick's wound.

"All right, let me put a towel or something around his thumb," she muttered. "Keep your hand in the water, okay?"

Joey nodded and did as she asked, while she searched for something to use. She found an old but clean hand towel in dark brown and figured the bloodstains wouldn't be too noticeable. "Okay, here, let's wrap this around your hand."

Joey sniffled again but allowed her to wrap the towel around his thumb. He turned toward the door, but his foot slipped in the slight puddle on the floor, making him wrinkle his nose in disgust.

She led the way into the kitchen, getting Joey settled in one of the kitchen chairs on the opposite side from where they'd been working on the timeline, while Nick brought over the first-aid kit.

"There's some triple antibiotic cream in here, too," he said, handing over the supplies.

"Good thing." She put a dollop of ointment over the cut and then carefully wrapped it in gauze and tapped it securely in place. "There, how's that?" she asked when she was finished.

Joey nodded. "Can you make the smell go away?" he asked.

She didn't quite understand why he was so upset about the smelly aftershave. It actually wasn't awful, the brand was well-known and obviously had remained popular over the years. She exchanged a perplexed glance at Nick. "Ah, sure, I'll clean up the bathroom floor, okay?"

"Are you hungry?" she heard Nick ask, as she walked down the hall to clean up the mess in the bathroom. "I can heat up some soup."

She filled the sink with soapy water and took yet another hand towel and did her best to clean up the spilled aftershave. But even after she finished, the scent still lingered.

There wasn't much she could do other than try to cut through the scent with a stronger cleaning agent.

She went back into the kitchen and found Nick heating up some chicken noodle soup for Joey. "Do you have any bleach or vinegar?" she asked in a low tone.

He grimaced. "I doubt it, but check in the pantry."

Calling the rough wooden open shelves a pantry was a bit of a misnomer, and she examined the contents but couldn't find anything she could use to help eliminate the odor.

"Don't worry," Nick said reassuringly. "I'm sure it will fade over time."

"No!" Joey shouted. "I don't like the smell! Make it go away!"

She rushed to Joey's side, wrapping her arms around her son. "Shh, sweetie, it's okay."

"Wait," Nick said, coming over to put a hand on her shoulder. "Does the smell remind you of something, Joey?" he asked.

Realization dawned slowly, and she pulled away just enough to look down at her son's face. Joey gazed up at her and then looked over at Nick. He didn't speak, but he slowly nodded his head yes.

Her heart clenched in her chest as the implication sank deep.

"What does the smell remind you of, Joey?" Nick asked gently. "Can you tell me?"

There was a long silence before Joey answered. "The bad man," he whispered.

"The bad man who put a hood over your head and carried you away after the crash?" Nick asked.

This time, her son shook his head no. "The other bad man. I didn't see him, but he spoke in a mean voice and he smelled bad. Like the bottle I accidently spilled in the bathroom."

The second bad man? For a moment Rachel couldn't move. Could barely comprehend what Joey meant.

Then she raised her head and locked gazes with Nick. And read the truth reflected in his eyes.

Forcing her to acknowledge that Joey had been somewhere near the man who'd arranged the kidnapping. Thinking back, she realized that their initial theory must have been correct. Morales had dumped the black truck shortly after the crash, catching a ride with someone else. The man who'd ordered the kidnapping in the first place.

Which meant her son might be able to recognize the

voice of the man who'd masterminded the entire operation.

Once they found him.

THIRTEEN

Nick tore his gaze from Rachel's when he heard the soup boiling. He rushed to the stove to remove the saucepan from the electric burner. "Soup's ready," he said.

Rachel shook her head, as if there was no way she'd be able to eat, but he knew they had to try to keep things normal, for Joey's sake. He filled several bowls with the steaming soup and carried them over to the table in two trips.

"Try to eat something, Joey," he urged. "You don't have to think about the bad man anymore."

"But I can still smell him," Joey whined.

"Try the soup, and I'll clean the floor again," Rachel murmured.

"After you eat something," Nick said, gesturing to the empty seat. She put a hand over her stomach but sat next to her son. He gave Rachel credit for trying, when she leaned over her bowl. "Hmm, smells good."

Joey leaned over his own soup and took a tentative sniff. The aroma of chicken soup seemed to appease him enough to take a sip. "Tastes good," he admitted.

Rachel took a sip, too. "Yes, it does."

They hadn't prayed, so Nick said a quick, silent prayer of thanks before taking a spoonful of his soup. The three of them sat in companionable silence as they enjoyed the simple meal. When Joey had finished, Rachel pushed away and carried her bowl to the sink. As soon as she'd rinsed her dishes, she returned to the bathroom.

Nick scrubbed a hand along the back of his neck, knowing that no matter how many times Rachel scrubbed the wooden floor, the scent of Wally's aftershave would linger.

In Joey's mind more so than in reality.

He quickly washed the dishes, while Joey went back to sit in front of the fire. The sad expression on the child's face made his heart ache. Sophie's life had been cut short by the car crash, but she'd always been a happy child. Loved school and had lots of friends. Both he and Becky had doted on their daughter. The thought of Sophie suffering the way Joey had made his chest hurt.

No matter how important this timeline was, he simply couldn't ignore Joey. Rachel returned to the room, looking dejected as she dropped onto the sofa beside her son.

"Hey, Joey, how would you like me to read the story of Christmas to you from the Bible?" he asked.

"The Bible has the story of Christmas in it?" Joey asked, his eyes wide with curiosity.

Rachel winced and he understood she was feeling guilty that Joey didn't know the real meaning of Christmas. "Yep, it sure does."

"Okay."

Nick picked up the Bible and settled onto the recliner. He opened his mother's Bible to the Gospel of Luke, Chapter 2 verse 7. "'And she brought forth her firstborn son and wrapped him in swaddling clothes and laid him in a manger; because there was no room for them in the inn.

"'And there were in the same country shepherds abiding in the field keeping watch over their flock by night. And, lo, the angel of the Lord came upon them and the glory of the Lord shone round about them; and they were sore afraid. And the angel said unto them, Fear not: for, behold, I bring you good tidings of great joy, which shall be to all people. For unto you is born this day in the city of David a Saviour, which is Christ the Lord.'"

He continued through verse twenty and when he finished reading, he was humbled to realize that both Joey and Rachel were staring at him, as if hanging on every word.

"And that is the true meaning of Christmas," he murmured, encouraged that this would be another step for both of them in their journey to believe.

Rachel loved listening to Nick read from the Bible, but she also felt bad that she hadn't taught Joey about God and the story of Jesus before now.

"That was a nice story," Joey said with a wide yawn.

She kissed the top of his head. "It was a wonderful story, wasn't it? I want you to think about God whenever you feel afraid, okay?"

"I will," Joey's voice was soft and sleepy.

Nick set the Bible aside and returned to the kitchen table to continue working on the timeline.

She needed to help Nick, but she didn't want to leave her son. It wasn't until Joey's head tipped to the side, indicating he'd fallen asleep, that she eased away and went to sit beside Nick.

"I suppose you think I'm a terrible mother," she said softly.

He glanced at her in surprise. "Why would I think that?"

The shame was almost too much to bear, but she forced herself to get this out in the open. "Because I didn't teach Joey about God. Because I didn't raise him to believe."

"It's never too late to start, Rachel," Nick murmured. He reached up and tucked a strand of her hair behind her ear. "And no, I don't think you're a terrible mother at all. If you weren't raised to believe in God, then it's no wonder you raised your son the same way."

She was silent for a long moment, wishing she dared to ask him to hold her. She thought back to her childhood. "I think my parents believed in God—at least, I remember going to church when I was young. But by the time I was Joey's age, we suddenly stopped going to church…and I pretty much forgot most of what I learned."

"Do you know why your parents stopped attending church?" he asked. The way he took her hand and interlaced his fingers with hers gave her the strength she needed.

"My mother lost her parents when I was nine, and they died about six months apart. And then when I was in high school, she was diagnosed with breast cancer. She passed away my freshman year in college." The pain of losing her mother had been terrible, but she and her father had clung together to get through it. Easy to look back now and piece together what had happened. The deaths of her grandparents had hit her mother hard, and maybe for some reason she'd pulled away from God. Her father, too, especially after losing her mother.

"I've seen that happen sometimes, where a sudden death causes a loss of faith," Nick said, giving her hand a gentle squeeze. "But to be honest, Rachel, those are the times when you should lean on God the most. I know it's hard—I struggled to keep my faith after my Becky and Sophie died."

"I can't imagine how difficult that must have been for you."

He was quiet for a moment. "Becky and I were high-school sweethearts so when I lost her, I felt like I lost my best friend. But now, after all these months, sometimes I have trouble remembering exactly what she looked like."

"Oh, Nick," she murmured. No one had ever loved her the way Nick had loved his wife.

He forced a smile. "I guess that might be God's way of making me realize I have a different path to follow. I know it's not easy, but if you open your heart to the Lord, you will be rewarded."

Maybe he was right. Certainly she'd felt some sense of peace when she'd prayed for Joey's safety. She stared down at their entwined fingers for a moment, feeling connected to Nick in a way she'd never experienced with Anthony.

The thought scared her. She didn't want to have feelings for Nick. Didn't want to open herself up to the possibility of rejection. She trusted Nick to keep her and Joey safe, but to trust him with her heart? That was asking too much.

The expression in his eyes when he spoke of his wife made her realize that he might not be ready for a relationship, either.

She took a deep breath and forced a smile. "So, let's get back to that timeline, huh?" she suggested, releasing his hand and turning toward the notebook paper he'd left on the table. "Where did we leave off?"

There was a troubled look in his eyes as he stared at her for a long moment before he sighed and turned toward the timeline. "We left off at the time of Josie Gardner's suicide or possible murder," he said.

She nodded. Was she wrong about what Nick wanted? Maybe, but, somehow, it was easier to talk about who might have kidnapped her son than her tangled feelings toward Nick.

* * *

The rest of the day passed by quicker than she would have imagined. Dark clouds rolled in, bringing the threat of a storm, but while the wind kicked up a bit, no snowflakes fell.

Nick walked around outside again, and she was reassured by his diligence. He continued to work on the timeline long after they'd taken a break for dinner.

She bowed her head while Nick thanked God once again for providing the hot meal and shelter. There weren't many options for dinner, so they had to eat more of the canned beef stew again but no one complained.

"Are we going to be home in time for Christmas?" Joey asked.

"Christmas is three days away, I'm sure we'll be home by then," she assured him.

Nick looked as if he didn't necessarily agree. "We can celebrate Christmas here, too, if we have to," he pointed out.

She knew he was right. "If we have to, we will," she agreed. "But hopefully things will get back to normal soon."

After dinner, Nick continued to work on the timeline. She found a game of checkers on the pantry shelf and played a few games with Joey to help keep him occupied. Soon Nick came over and asked if he could play the winner, and she was truly disappointed when Joey beat her.

As she watched Nick and Joey play, she was struck by how easy it was to feel they were a family. Had she been wrong to warn Nick to keep his distance? He was everything a role model should be: kind and considerate... strong yet gentle. What a wonderful husband and father he must have been. So different from her ex.

Joey won again, and he let out a whoop. She had to

make sure her yearning for a family of her own wasn't visible on her face when she gave Joey a high five.

Several games later, after Joey had yawned for the fifth time in a row, she deemed it time for bed. "Say good-night to Nick," she reminded her son.

"Good night, Nick, you're the best dad ever," Joey said.

Her breath froze in her chest and she stared at her son in horror. Why had he said that? It was as if she'd somehow projected her secret wishes into her son.

"You're welcome, Joey," Nick said thickly. "Get some sleep, now, okay?"

"Come on, Joey," she mumbled, completely mortified by the turn of events. "Good night, Nick."

"Good night." Nick gave her a searching look, which she avoided meeting head-on—too afraid he'd see the same sentiment in her eyes. He picked up the Bible and as much as she was tempted to stay and listen while he read some more she had no choice but to go with her son, who was still afraid of the dark. Besides, she couldn't imagine trying to explain why Joey had called him the best dad ever.

She'd never been more acutely aware of how her son had been impacted by growing up without a father. Had he been looking for a surrogate father this whole time?

Was it any wonder he'd latched on to Nick?

She and Joey took turns in the bathroom, the scent of the aftershave far less obvious now, though still lingering in the air. Joey wrinkled his nose but otherwise seemed fine as he crawled under the pile of quilts on the bed.

Joey immediately fell asleep but, just like the night before, her mind refused to settle. She tried to remember some of the Bible phrases Nick had read but could only recall a line or two.

She kept replaying the moment that Joey had called

Nick the best dad ever. She hoped Nick didn't put too much importance on what her son had said. The way she already had.

At some point she must have dozed, because a noise startled her awake. Another wild animal moving through the woods? She stayed perfectly still, straining to listen.

After several moments, she crawled from beneath the quilts and moved silently over to the window overlooking the back side of the cabin. There weren't any stars out as they were well hidden behind a blanket of clouds.

She heard it again, the same thunk that had woken her. Did animals make that kind of sound? Somehow she doubted it. She stuffed her feet into her athletic shoes and cautiously made her way down the hall to find Nick.

Nick shot upright when he felt a hand on his arm. "What?" he asked harshly, blinking the sleep from his eyes as he gazed up at Rachel.

"Get up, I think I heard something outside," she whispered.

His pulse kicked into triple digits and he swung around to put his feet on the floor. "Are you sure?" he asked in a low, raspy voice as he quickly slid his feet into his shoes and tied the laces.

"I don't think it was an animal," she said, her eyes wide with fear. "It was a thunking noise and I heard it twice."

Nick wrestled with guilt, knowing that he should have taken Jonah's advice and found a new place to stay. But it was too late for self-recriminations. He needed to get Rachel and Joey safely out of the cabin. "Wake up Joey and make sure he's wearing his winter jacket and his shoes, okay?"

"Okay." To her credit, Rachel didn't panic and went to do exactly as she was told.

He used the poker to break up the remains of the fire, and closed the iron doors on the fireplace, to help douse the flames and eliminate even that small bit of light. The room was plunged into darkness and it took him a minute for his eyes to adjust. He tucked his weapon in his shoulder harness and then went over to peer out the large picture window.

He couldn't see much, but that was okay, since it helped keep them hidden, as well. When Rachel and Joey returned, he crossed over to them. "Be as quiet as possible, okay? Follow me…we're going outside."

Rachel snagged his arm. "Aren't we safer in here?"

"No, we're boxed in. Try to trust me on this, Rachel."

He could barely see her in the darkness. "I do trust you, Nick."

Whether or not he deserved her trust remained to be seen. But they had to move, so he simply led the way over to the front door. As quietly as possible, he eased back the dead bolt, although the click was louder than he liked. Without wasting time, he opened the door and cast a quick glance around the clearing.

Joey and Rachel crowded behind him, waiting silently for his direction. He took a moment to pray for their safety, before guiding them out onto the front porch, keeping as close to the cabin as possible.

Rachel sent Joey first, and then followed from behind. He didn't have to tell her to make sure the door didn't slam shut as she softly closed it before making her way over to where they stood. The night was so cold they could see their breath in the air, and the frozen leaves and brush would make it far more difficult to move silently through the woods.

First, he needed to figure out which was the best direction to go. He waited for a long moment, listening to the sounds of the night. It was too cold for any insects, but at least the wind had died down.

As much as he wanted to use the car to escape, he couldn't deny the possibility that the intruder had already found it and disabled it. At least, that's what he would have done.

No, their best bet was to stay hidden in the woods for as long as possible. He didn't dare use his cell phone yet, as the light from the screen would only broadcast their position to whoever was out there.

The closest grouping of evergreen trees was to the left in the nine-o'clock position, so he bent down to whisper in Rachel's ear. "Follow me to the evergreens."

He could feel her head nod, her hair brushing his face. Satisfied, he inched across the porch, praying the boards wouldn't creak.

The trek to the group of evergreens seemed to take forever, but the moment they reached them, he felt himself relax. Thank goodness they were all wearing dark clothing, and, without the moon, he hoped their pale faces wouldn't attract too much attention.

"Stay here, I'm going to take a look around," he whispered again, right next to Rachel's ear.

"No, wait," she grabbed his arm in a tense grip. "I smell smoke."

He paused and tried to estimate how long the scent of smoke would linger in the air after he'd put out the fire inside the cabin.

"There!" Rachel whispered urgently, pointing to an area behind the cabin.

He saw what had captured her attention. Orange flames flickering in the darkness.

Fire!

FOURTEEN

Rachel stared at the small flickering flames in horror. The kidnapper must have found them. Who else would do such a thing? She knew Nick thought Morales had been ordered to kill her and Joey, but they'd managed to get away. The kidnapper must have come back to finish the job. And what if she hadn't woken up from the thunking noise? Would they have died inside the cabin? Had that been the kidnappers' plan all along?

Cold fear slid down her spine.

Thank You, Lord, for saving us!

"I think the outhouse might be on fire," Nick whispered. "And if that's the case, I'm afraid the fire will spread to the cabin." He paused, looking out over the trees. "Looks like the wind is blowing north. We'll need to head south so that we're heading in the opposite direction."

"Okay." She wasn't about to argue. Joey's hand was trembling inside of hers, from the cold or fear or both. She tightened her grip reassuringly, knowing she'd do whatever was necessary to keep him safe. "Lead the way."

Nick stayed between the trees, moving slowly and silently away from the cabin. She did her best to follow in his footsteps, but it seemed like twigs snapped loudly beneath her feet and her clothing brushed and snagged against the tree branches with every step. The cold night air blew sharp against her face, but she knew the fire was the bigger threat compared to the stinging cold.

Although both could be deadly.

They hadn't made it very far when a loud crack echoed through the night.

"Get down," Nick urged.

Someone was shooting at them! She instinctively dropped low, ducking behind a tree while covering Joey's body with hers, protecting him the best she could.

They waited motionless for what seemed like an hour but was likely only a few minutes. There was no further gunfire and she wasn't sure if that was good news or bad.

Was the kidnapper tracking them through the woods right now?

"We need to split up," Nick whispered, his mouth close to her ear.

"No! We need to stick together!" she whispered back.

"Listen to me." Nick's tone was harsh. "We need to get help. You and Joey are going to take my phone and head southeast. When you're far enough away, call 911."

"I don't even know where we are," she murmured anxiously.

"The address here is 472 and Highway MM."

She silently repeated it to herself, committing the address to memory.

"I'm going to draw the gunman away from you and Joey. So you need to get moving, now."

"I still think you should come with us," she whispered again. She couldn't help remembering the last time she'd tried to save her son by sending him out of the mangled wreck of their car only to watch him be captured and kidnapped. What if the same thing happened to Nick?

"Go!" he said, and he turned and fired in the direction

from which the gunshot had originated. "I'll hold him off long enough for help to arrive."

She hesitated, torn between two impossible choices. She desperately wanted to get Joey to safety, but she also didn't want to leave Nick, unable to bear the thought of anything happening to him. Yet she knew her son was depending on her so she did as Nick asked, staying low and easing back into the cover of the trees, keeping Joey close to her side.

Joey must have understood the acute need for silence since he didn't say a word as they made their way through a particularly thick grove. When they'd gone about twenty yards, she crouched behind a large tree and took out Nick's phone. She unzipped her coat, using the edges of her jacket to help hide the unmistakable glow of the phone screen as she called 911. The operator seemed to take forever to answer, and when she finally did, she hoped she remembered everything correctly.

"Please send help," Rachel said urgently. "Someone is shooting at us and he's also started a fire. The address is 472 and Highway MM."

"Are you hurt?" the dispatcher asked.

"Not yet, but please hurry!" There was another loud crack followed by a cry of pain and she instinctively clutched Joey close, using her body as a shield to cover her son's.

Even though she'd dropped the phone, she could still hear the dispatcher's voice talking. She frantically searched the ground with her fingertips. The snow was cold, making her fingers numb, but she eventually found the phone and powered it off.

"Are you all right?" she asked Joey softly, fearing that the kidnapper had seen them despite her efforts to keep the screen hidden from view. "He didn't hit you, did he?"

"No, I'm not hurt," Joey whispered. "I'm scared."

Her heart ached for him. "I know, but remember what Nick taught us? God is watching over us. God will keep us safe."

Joey nodded solemnly. "I'm going to keep praying."

Tears pricked her eyes. "Me, too." She gave her son a quick hug and then glanced back over her shoulder searching for Nick. Panic swelled in the back of her throat when she couldn't see him. What if he'd been hit? The orange glow from the fire was brighter, indicating that it was beginning to spread.

Dear Lord, please keep Nick safe! Please keep us all safe!

"I smell the bad man," Joey whimpered.

Since all she could smell was smoke, she didn't necessarily believe him. But at that moment, a bright spotlight illuminated the woods, blinding her. The light was only forty feet away! She shoved Joey behind her and tried to edge closer behind an evergreen tree.

"Stay right where you are, Rachel!" a voice shouted. "If you move, I'll keep shooting."

She froze at the familiar voice. *Gerry?* Abruptly, all the puzzle pieces clicked into place. Gerry Ashton always wore strong aftershave, very similar to the kind Joey had spilled in the cabin. And now she clearly recognized his voice.

Her mind wrestled helplessly with the truth. The man she'd trusted more than anyone else in the company had been the one who'd hired Morales to kidnap Joey. Had Gerry also kept her son locked up in his basement? The thought made her furious. To think she'd played right into his hands by begging him to buy her shares of the company. Had he sent the letters, too, pretending to be part of the Mafia?

Gerry was one of the few who'd known about how her father had helped her escape Anthony. Maybe he'd used the Mafia link on purpose to scare her. She wasn't sure if he'd killed Josie Gardner, too, or if the researcher had really committed suicide, but it was clear he intended to kill her and Joey, right here, right now.

Everything suddenly made sense in a sick, horrible way.

How could she have been so blind? So stupid? How could she not have known? Edith must have suspected something wasn't right with Gerry, which was why she'd quit.

She should have asked her assistant for more information. But it was too late now. She forced herself to keep facing Gerry even as she whispered to her son. "Stay hidden behind the tree."

Joey soundlessly moved deeper into the branches. She lifted her arm to shield her eyes against the glare. "Don't shoot!" she shouted. "I'm not armed."

"No, but your boyfriend was." She tried not to react to Gerry's use of the past tense in reference to Nick. "You and Joey need to come back to the cabin, Rachel. Right now," Gerry demanded.

The cabin? Was he crazy? No way was she doing that. What was Gerry thinking to suggest she take her son anywhere near a burning building? If the cabin wasn't on fire yet, it soon would be. She'd rather take her chances getting lost in the woods. But how long could she hold him off? Gerry must know that she'd already called for help, especially if he caught a glimpse of the glow from Nick's cell phone.

And where was Nick?

"Why?" she asked, stalling for time. "Give me one good reason why I should make it easy for you to kill us?"

Another crack shattered the night and she gasped and ducked, half expecting to feel the searing pain from being hit by a bullet.

"That was just a warning shot," Gerry snarled. "Next time, I'll make that kid of yours an orphan."

She sucked in a harsh breath, feeling trapped. If they tried to run, Gerry could easily follow them with the light. She had no idea where Nick was, and she prayed he wasn't lying in the woods, bleeding to death. As the seconds stretched into a full minute, she wondered why Gerry didn't just shoot her and get it over with. What did he hope to gain in this weird cat-and-mouse game?

The glow of the fire burned bright behind Gerry, and suddenly it dawned on her that Gerry wanted them to burn inside the cabin. Maybe he thought that would make their deaths look like a tragic accident. Bullet wounds would be too obvious.

Grimly, she realized he had no intention of letting any of them live through this.

"Why are you doing this, Gerry? You have the money! And the company!" She thought it was best to keep him talking.

"Your father promised the company to me! That idiot Morales was supposed to kill you both. You're too smart for your own good, Rachel. I knew you'd figure out that I was the one behind this sooner or later."

She wasn't about to admit she hadn't realized that until right now. "Why did you decide to take over the company now? Why not back when my dad died?"

"Because Nancy was threatening to divorce me," Gerry said in a vicious tone. "I signed a prenup so I get nothing. I needed that company. And you were going to give all that money to settle the lawsuit!" He released a ragged breath. "You didn't deserve to keep it. But just taking over the company wasn't enough. Everyone kept asking about what it would take to bring you back. Leaving me no choice but to get rid of you both once and for all."

He was crazy, no doubt about it. How were they going to get away?

Another gunshot echoed, and this time she saw the spotlight waver, as if Gerry had ducked.

Nick! Nick was alive!

The next gunshot hit the spotlight dead on, shattering the bulb. But even with the spotlight off, there was too much light from the roaring fire that quickly engulfed the dry timber of the log cabin.

Rachel took the opportunity to move from their current location, urging Joey to stay shielded behind her as they darted around more trees. But then she froze when another crack of gunfire shattered the night.

She whipped around and, from the glow of the fire behind her, Rachel watched Gerry's dark shadow stagger and then finally go down.

She hesitated, torn by indecision. Was Gerry dead? Or at least hurt badly enough that he couldn't keep shooting?

And where was Nick?

She crouched beside her son for long, agonizing moments. She didn't want to risk Joey's life by taking him over to find Nick, but at the same time, she didn't want to leave him here, alone.

"Rachel?" Nick's voice was weak. "Are you and Joey all right?"

Her head shot over to the right, her eyes trying to pierce the darkness. "Yes, we're fine," she called back. "But where are you?"

"Over here." Nick's voice was definitely lacking strength—she could barely hear him over the roaring of the fire. "I've been hit."

* * *

Nick kept his eyes glued to where Gerry Ashton's body lay sprawled on the ground. If the man so much as twitched he'd shoot him again.

His eyes blurred and he blinked in an effort to bring the world back into focus. The smoke was getting thicker and he knew he couldn't stay too long. His left arm felt like it was on fire, and the loss of blood was making him dizzy. Figured he'd got hit in the same area as when they'd saved Joey during the money exchange.

Only this time, the injury was much worse. Propped against the tree, he tugged on the string from the hooded sweatshirt he wore, until it came free. Using the string like a tourniquet, he awkwardly wrapped it around his arm and used his teeth to tie it tight. He wanted to drag himself over to make sure Gerry was really dead, but on the off chance that the guy was only pretending in an effort to draw his prey closer, Nick decided it was safer to stay far away.

Where were the cops and the firefighters? He'd heard Rachel calling 911, so he knew reinforcements had to be on the way. Wally's cabin wasn't going to survive the fire, but he was more concerned about the fire spreading through the woods. Drought conditions had hit hard the previous summer, and despite the thin layer of snow covering the ground, he thought the trees were burning too fast.

As if on cue, a large pine tree to the right of the outhouse went up in flames, the tiny needles glowing red as they burned. Knowing they didn't have a lot of time left to get somewhere safe, he forced himself upright, using the tree for support.

"Nick!" He was caught off guard when Joey came running toward him. He opened his mouth to yell at the boy to stay down, when he realized that Gerry hadn't moved, not even an inch despite the fire growing closer.

Joey's second bad guy was finally dead.

"Hey, it's okay," he managed when Joey flung his arms around his waist, burying his face in his stomach. "I'm okay."

"I thought you were dead," the child sobbed.

Rachel looked upset at Joey's statement. "Where are you hit?" she asked.

"My left arm same as before, but never mind that, now. We need to get as far away from the fire as we can. It's been so dry up here that the fire will soon burn out of control."

"Lean on me," Rachel offered, slipping her shoulder beneath his injured arm and sliding her other hand around his waist.

He didn't like the fact that he was so weak that he had little choice but to allow her to help him. Surprisingly, Joey went around on the other side of him, and together they moved as quickly as possible away from the fire.

"Joey, can you find the gravel driveway?" he asked, since his vision was blurry again.

"I think so," Joey said. "This way!"

The three of them stumbled toward the direction of the driveway with a deep sense of urgency. Nick refused to look back over his shoulder, too afraid he'd see the fire nipping hotly at their heels.

There was another loud whooshing sound, and he knew another tree had gone up in flames. They had to get out of here, and fast!

When the gravel crunched beneath his feet, he let out a sigh of relief. Joey's sense of direction had been perfect. They continued moving as fast as they could, putting more distance between them and the raging fire. The smoke was still hanging thick between the trees.

He coughed and a spear of pain shot down his arm. He ignored it, more concerned when he heard Rachel and Joey coughing, too. How much time did they have before they succumbed to smoke inhalation?

Dear Lord, show us the way to safety.

"Come on, Nick, don't give up now!" Rachel urged in a raspy voice. Obviously the smoke was getting to her, too. And what about Joey? He was so young that Nick was afraid it wouldn't take long for the smoke to damage the boy's lungs.

He hadn't realized his steps were lagging behind, and he forced himself to move faster for both Rachel and Joey's sake. They deserved a chance to get out of here, alive.

Within five minutes, Nick practically fell over the hood of the car, and he slumped against the metal frame gratefully. For the first time in hours, he allowed himself a flash of hope. "Maybe we can drive out of here," he proposed, fumbling in his pockets for the keys. He found them and tugged them free. "Think you're up to it?"

"I'll try," Rachel said, jumping eagerly at his suggestion. She stepped forward to take the keys, and she opened the driver's door. But before she could slide inside, a man appeared out of the woods, holding a rifle.

"Don't move," he barked loudly.

"Karl!" Rachel exclaimed. Then, in a move that was so subtle Nick almost missed it, she pushed Joey behind her, probably intending for him to climb into the safety of the car. "What are you doing? Why do you have a gun?"

Karl? Nick stared in shocked surprise as he realized that the stranger was Dr. Karl Errol, the researcher he'd suspected was secretly working for Global Pharmaceuticals. His instincts must have been right on. The researcher must have purposefully set up Rachel's company to fail. But seeing him here, as if he'd teamed up with Gerry Ashton, didn't make much sense. Why would the researcher who'd tried to destroy Rachel's company work alongside Ashton, who clearly wanted to take over the company himself?

He didn't know for sure, but obviously Errol wasn't messing around. The way he held the rifle in his hands told Nick he wouldn't hesitate to kill them.

FIFTEEN

Nick gritted his teeth as Rachel tried to reason with Karl Errol. "Gerry is dead, Karl. You don't have to do this. Just let us go."

"I'm not working for Gerry," Errol said finally. "And my boss isn't going to accept failure."

Nick tried to think of a way out of this mess. But he couldn't come up with a safe option. Granted, he still had his weapon, but he didn't dare try to take Errol out while the guy held the rifle pointed directly at Rachel. Maybe if he was at full strength he could rush the guy, catching him off guard.

But he'd lost too much blood to risk it. He was far more likely to fall flat on his face before he reached Errol. He seriously felt as if a strong breeze would blow him over.

"Who's your boss, Karl? Why are you doing this?" Rachel asked, taking a step toward him. It was all Nick could do not to shout at her to stay back. "Have you really been working for Global Pharmaceuticals this whole time? Why? Why did you hate me so much you wanted to put me out of business?"

Errol shook his head, as if waging an inner war with himself. "I didn't have a choice. I followed Ashton here and waited, hoping he'd take care of things for me. But he botched the job. Leaving me no choice."

Nick tried to take heart in knowing the guy hadn't shot them yet, even though he'd had time. Maybe there was a way to get through to him.

But how?

"There's no point in trying to reason with him, Rachel. He doesn't care about anyone but himself. I told you he killed Josie Gardener," Nick told her in a scathing tone. "She stumbled upon the truth and was going to let you know what she'd found out. So he killed her and set the whole thing up to look like a suicide."

"No!" Errol shouted. "I loved Josie! I would never hurt her. But she didn't love me."

A cold chill snaked down his spine. Now they were getting somewhere. "Who did she love, Karl?" he asked mildly.

"Ashton." Errol's tone reeked of loathing. "But that jerk didn't deserve her love. He had an affair with her even though he had no intention of leaving his rich wife."

"Ashton is dead. He won't hurt anyone ever again, Karl." Rachel's tone was soothing. She took another small step forward, holding her hand out. "Just put down the gun and we'll work this through, okay?"

"Stop!" he screamed. "You can't fix this. Don't you understand? I did it for Josie! I secretly worked for Global to make enough money to compete with Ashton. I told her I could afford to buy her nice things, and take her to fancy places. But she didn't care! She wanted to live in sin as Ashton's mistress rather than to give me the chance to make her happy."

Slowly the picture became clear. "Are you saying that Ashton killed Josie?" Rachel asked incredulously.

"Yes, because she was pressuring him to leave his wife.

Maybe he was afraid she'd tell his wife about the affair. And if he divorced his wife he'd lose all the big bucks he'd gotten accustomed to spending. But none of that matters anymore." He blew out an angry breath. "I'm glad Ashton's dead. You saved me the trouble of killing him. But, unfortunately, I have no choice but to kill you, too." Errol tightened his grip on the gun.

"Wait! You do have a choice. What if I promise not to press charges against you?" Rachel asked in a desperate tone. "Then will you put the gun down? I promise I won't turn you in to the authorities. All I want is to go home with my son."

For a moment Nick thought she may have convinced Errol with her heartfelt plea. But then Karl slowly brought the rifle up to shoulder height and bent his head forward as if to take aim.

"No!" Joey came charging out from the back end of the car carrying a thick tree branch. His shout startled Karl enough that he jerked around toward Joey's direction, shooting wildly.

"Joey," Rachel shrieked.

The boy didn't stop. He must not have been hit by the wild shot, because he swung the tree branch with all his might, aiming at Karl's knees.

Nick made a split-second decision, gathering every ounce of his strength to propel himself across the small clearing toward Errol. As the guy fell down, howling in agony, Nick kicked the rifle up and out of the way and threw himself on top of the researcher.

Within moments, Rachel had the rifle safely in her hands. "Get out of the way," she shouted.

Nick rolled off Errol and she quickly brought the heavy stock down on Errol's head, knocking him unconscious.

The sound of sirens, hopefully from both ambulances

and fire trucks, echoed through the night. Finally, there was hope that help was soon to arrive. He didn't have the strength to move, so he stayed right where he was.

"Joey, are you all right?" Rachel asked.

"Yes. I was afraid he was going to shoot you." Nick heard the boy's footsteps creeping forward. "Nick? Are you okay?"

He tried to crack a smile. "Fine, buddy. Just tired. I'm going to rest for a minute, okay?"

Rachel dropped to her knees beside him. "Come on, Nick," she pleaded. "You can't stay here—you need to get up! Karl isn't dead and we can't be here when he wakes up."

The panic in her tone pierced his soul, so he pushed himself upright with his good arm, biting back a groan of pain. He was still dizzy and knew he'd already lost too much blood. The artery in his arm must be nicked.

Somehow, with Rachel and Joey's help, he managed to get back on his feet. The three of them staggered toward the car and he leaned against the frame gratefully. There was no telling how long Errol would remain unconscious, so he knew they had to get out of there, and quickly. "Rachel, do you still have the car keys? Let's see if we can drive out of here."

"Good idea." Rachel slid behind the wheel and jammed the key into the ignition. He closed his eyes in despair when he heard a *click-click* as she attempted to start the car.

"I'm sorry, Nick," Rachel lamented, and got out of the car. "Either Karl or Gerry must have done something to the engine."

He opened his eyes and nodded wearily. "I shouldn't be surprised. Guess we'll have to try and make it to the highway by walking."

"Nick, you're bleeding!" Joey exclaimed.

He glanced down and winced when he saw the dark stain of blood smeared across the palm of Joey's hand. "Yeah, but it's just a scratch," he said, downplaying his injury. "I'll be fine as soon as the ambulance gets here."

Joey still looked horrified, and he hated knowing he was causing the child to be afraid again. Hadn't the poor kid been through enough? He'd never forget the way Joey went charging after Errol with the tree branch. The kid was a true hero. "Listen, Joey, can you hear the sirens? The police will be here soon. Everything's going to be all right."

"Let's go, Nick." Rachel slid her arm around his waist, putting her shoulder under his arm to help support him. He silently prayed for strength as they made their way down the rest of the gravel driveway. The hazy smoke made it difficult to see and to breathe. The three of them coughed as they walked. He could barely see a few feet in front of his face, so he had no way of knowing if they were anywhere close to the highway.

After about ten minutes, he could feel his strength waning, even with Rachel trying to take most of his weight. He stumbled on a large rock and knew he was going to fall. Instantly, he let go of both Rachel and Joey so he wouldn't take them down with him. He groaned loudly when he hit the ground, hard. For a moment everything went black and he stopped fighting, stopped struggling, welcoming the darkness.

"Nick! Are you all right?" From far away, he could feel someone shaking him and calling his name. Rachel? He didn't have the strength to reassure her.

Once he'd prayed for the Lord to take him so he could be with his wife and daughter again. But it hadn't been his time. Was God going to take him now? Just when he'd found Rachel? He didn't want to leave Rachel and Joey, but he didn't have the strength to fight anymore.

"Take me home, Lord," he whispered. "I'm ready to come home."

"Nick!" Rachel tried not to panic as she stripped away his coat so she could look at his arm. Not that she would be able to see much in the darkness.

"Is Nick going to die?" Joey asked, his voice trembling with fear.

"Not if I can help it," she muttered. Nick's jacket wouldn't come off and she soon realized he'd tied a string around the upper part of his left arm in an attempt to stop the bleeding.

"No, God wants me home…." he muttered, weakly pushing her hands away.

Rachel couldn't believe Nick was just going to give up. She remembered him mentioning his wife and daughter were up in heaven. Was he willing to give up his life in order to be with them again? Didn't she and Joey mean anything to him?

Maybe not, but that was too bad. She wasn't ready to let him go. She untied the string and yanked the jacket sleeve off. His blood-soaked sweatshirt confirmed her worst fears.

He was hit badly, far worse than he'd let on.

Working quickly, she felt for the worst part of the injury, trying not to wince when her fingers sank into the open wound. Once she'd found it, she retied the string around his arm above the injured area. What else could she use to stop the bleeding? She shrugged out of her coat, took off her sweatshirt and then put her coat back on. Using the sleeve of her sweatshirt, figuring it was cleaner than the hood, she balled it up and pressed it against the gouged area across Nick's biceps.

"Come on, Nick. Help me out here," she urged as she leaned all her weight against him, hoping to slow the blood loss. But Nick didn't move, didn't so much as flutter an eyelash.

"Wake up, Nick," Joey said, shaking Nick's other arm. "You have to wake up!"

The sounds of sirens grew louder. "Hang in there, Nick. The ambulance is almost here!"

Still, Nick didn't respond, not even when the ambulance and the firefighters arrived. Two paramedics came over to help Nick while the rest of the firefighters headed in with a huge water truck to the wooded area to douse the fire.

"He's lost a lot of blood," Rachel cautioned, when the two paramedics nudged her aside.

"Let's get an IV in, stat!" the female paramedic said curtly.

"I've got it," the younger man replied. "Fluids wide open until we can get the O neg blood flowing."

"His blood pressure is low—I'll get the packed red blood cells out of the ambulance," the woman continued. She darted away and returned with a small cooler less than two minutes later. She quickly opened the cooler and took out what looked like packages of blood.

Rachel kept Joey close to her side as they watched the two paramedics work on Nick. Once they had the blood infusing into his veins, they brought over a gurney and began to strap him securely onto it.

"Could we go with you? Please?" Rachel asked, stepping forward. "Our car has been tampered with and we don't have a ride out of here. There's also a man who tried to kill us still back in the woods."

The two paramedics grimaced. "I'm sorry, but that's against the rules," the younger man said.

"Besides, the police will want to talk to you, especially if there's still a threat here in the area," the female paramedic added kindly. "We're taking him to Madison General Hospital and I'm sure one of the officers will give you a ride."

Her heart sank, but she also knew they were right. She had little choice but to stand there with her arm around Joey and watch as they bundled Nick into the ambulance.

"Do you think God will listen if we pray for Nick?" Joey asked, after the paramedic jumped into the driver's seat, started the engine and pulled out onto the highway.

She gathered him close and nodded. "Absolutely, Joey," she responded. "Dear Lord, we ask You to please keep Nick safe in Your care. Amen."

"Amen," Joey echoed.

Tears burned her eyes as she realized that no matter what happened moving forward, her son was going to be hurt by Nick's leaving. Because he already cared about Nick, already saw him as some sort of surrogate father.

And she couldn't blame him, because if she were honest with herself, she'd admit she was falling for Nick, too. Maybe he didn't feel the same way, but she couldn't imagine a life without him.

Please, Lord, let him live!

"What do you mean you can't find Karl?" Rachel asked, her tone rising incredulously. With the smoke growing thicker in the woods despite the firefighters' attempt to douse the raging flames, the police officer had stashed her and Joey in the squad car while they went searching for the scientist. "He was lying on the ground about twenty feet away from the car. You found the car, right?"

"Yes, ma'am, we found the vehicle. And we looked all over but didn't find any sign of the research doctor or the weapon." The tall, dark-haired police officer had introduced himself as Sean McCarthy.

Rachel shivered and hugged Joey. The thought of Karl Errol being out on the loose in the woods with his rifle wasn't at all reassuring. She wished now that she had taken the gun with her. She glanced through the passenger-side window, hoping that Karl had taken the opportunity to escape rather than to seek revenge.

She could still barely comprehend that Gerry Ashton had decided to kill her and Joey as retaliation for her father giving her the company. And because he thought she was onto him. She felt sick to her stomach, thinking about how she'd been duped by the man she'd trusted.

Once again, her instincts had led her wrong.

"You say you believe Karl Errol was secretly working for Global Pharmaceuticals?" Officer McCarthy asked.

"That's what he admitted to. I'm still having trouble understanding how two people hated me enough to try and kill me."

"Can't say that I have much experience with corporate espionage," McCarthy admitted.

"Me, either," she murmured. She didn't want to think about greed and corruption anymore. Right now, she wanted to see Nick. To make sure he was all right.

"Officer McCarthy, will you please take us to Madison General Hospital?" she asked, willing to beg if necessary. It seemed as if hours had passed since the ambulance had driven away with Nick. She wanted nothing more than to get far away from this place where Nick had almost died and where she and Joey had feared for their lives, too.

"We've given you our statements. It's not like we can't discuss this in more detail later, right?"

Officer McCarthy hesitated but then nodded. "All right. We'll head over to the hospital. If Detective Butler is awake, I'll get his statement, as well."

Her shoulders slumped with relief. She didn't bother telling the officer that the likelihood of Nick answering any questions was slim to none. She wouldn't be at all surprised to find that Nick was already in surgery, having the injury to his arm repaired. If he survived long enough to get to surgery.

No, she refused to believe the worst. God was surely watching over Nick. He'd been a good Christian his entire life.

She didn't even want to consider the alternative. That God would take Nick home to be with his wife and daughter.

The ride to the hospital didn't take too long, although Joey was half asleep by the time they arrived. With Officer McCarthy as their escort, they made their way to the waiting area and were given a quick update about Nick's condition.

"Detective Butler is still in surgery," the woman behind the desk informed them. "But he should be out soon. Now tell me what relation are you to the patient?"

Rachel swallowed hard. "I— We're good friends. He, uh, has sisters, but I don't know how to get in touch with them." She knew he had parents, although she wasn't sure how to contact them, either. How was it that she was more familiar with the names of his dead wife and daughter than his living family members?

Maybe calling herself a friend was stretching the truth. She was just a woman who'd needed Nick's protection and his expertise. Nothing more, nothing less.

The kiss they'd shared didn't mean anything. And she'd be stupid to think it had.

She and Joey went to sit down, and soon Joey was snuggled against her, falling asleep. She tucked Officer McCarthy's business card in her pocket and let her head drop back against the wall.

As soon as they found Karl Errol, this nightmare would really be over. She and Joey could go back home to their normal lives. Granted there would still be some red tape before the money was returned her, but she was convinced it would all work out.

She wondered how long Nick would have to stay off duty as a result of his gunshot wound and hoped it wouldn't be too long. Grimly, she realized there was no way she'd ever be able to repay him for everything he'd done for her and for Joey.

He'd put his life and his career on the line for them. More than once. Without Nick's help she wouldn't have managed to get Joey back.

Not only had he kept them both safe, but he'd also taught them to believe in God.

Yet all she could offer in return was to pray for him to recover with the full use of his arm.

"Ms. Simon?" A hand shook her awake and she blinked, momentarily confused as to where she was. Then she recognized the unmistakable antiseptic smell of a hospital.

"What?" She winced when her neck muscles tightened painfully as she turned toward the hospital employee. "Nick? Is he out of surgery?"

"Yes. The doctor is on his way down to talk to you."

Joey was still asleep beside her and she tried not to wake him as she eased away. She rubbed her hands over her gritty eyes and was surprised to find that the sky out-side was beginning to lighten.

A harried surgeon wearing green scrubs came into the room. "Ms. Simon? I'm Dr. Wagner. Detective Butler's surgery went well. We were able to save his arm, although it was touch and go for a while as his brachial artery was injured. He's just about finished in the recovery area and then will be sent to the ICU where they can watch him more closely." He smiled compassionately. "You'll be able to visit him in about forty-five minutes or so."

Her mind was spinning with all the information he'd told her. Although she was certainly relieved that Nick had made it through the surgery, she still couldn't help worrying. "Is there any way he could still lose his arm?" she asked.

For a moment hesitation shadowed the doctor's eyes. "We're going to keep a close eye on his circulation. If there's any change, we'll take him back to surgery. We'll know more after twenty-four hours or so."

Rachel nodded to indicate she understood. "Thank you," she whispered.

The doctor flashed a brief smile before he turned and left. Joey woke up, complaining that he was hungry. Un-fortunately, Rachel didn't have any money on her, not even an ID. They'd left everything they had in the cabin, which was likely burned beyond repair by now.

"Here, these are meal passes for the cafeteria," the woman behind the desk said, offering up two small plas-tic cards. "They're worth about five dollars each."

"Thank you so much," Rachel murmured, taking them gratefully. Getting something to eat would help pass the time until she and Joey could visit Nick in the ICU.

It was closer to an hour later before the ICU called down for them. She held tightly on to Joey's hand as they went into the critical-care area. Nick's room was the second door on the left, so they cautiously approached.

"He looks bad, Mom," Joey choked out, his eyes filling with tears. "He looks like he's going to die."

"Joey, listen to me. The doctor said Nick is stable. He wouldn't lie to us. It's just that Nick is connected to lots of machines right now." She did her best to soothe her son, although she felt just as awful seeing Nick like this.

Rachel stepped forward and took Nick's uninjured hand in hers. "Nick, it's me, Rachel. Joey is here, too. The doctor said you're going to be fine. Do you hear me? You're going to be just fine."

Nick's eyelids fluttered for a moment and he looked directly at her. She smiled. "They said your arm should heal. I don't want you to worry about anything, okay?"

"Where am I?" he asked, his eyes full of confusion.

She tried not to let her fear show. "You're at the hospital in Madison. You just had surgery on your arm."

"But I—can't feel my arm," he whispered in agony.

"Your arm is right here." She patted the heavily bandaged limb gently. "The doctor said there's a good chance you'll make a full recovery." She made sure her tone was encouraging.

"I can't—" Nick stopped, closed his eyes, and turned his head away as if shutting her out.

Rejection seared her soul and she stepped back, keeping her expression neutral for Joey's sake. She didn't want to leave, but he'd made his feelings clear. Did she really think he was going to lose his arm? Where was his faith in God?

She didn't want to think that Nick preferred to be alone through this difficult time, but really, how much did she truly know about him? Maybe he only wanted his family here. Like his parents or his sisters.

She was just a woman he'd gone out of his way to help. Obviously, there was nothing more for her to do here.

She took a deep breath, trying to ease her heartache. This was why she'd avoided becoming emotionally involved. Only this time, she wasn't the only one who would be hurt.

Joey's heart would be broken, as well.

SIXTEEN

Nick fought the rising sense of despair. The doctor had told him that they'd saved his arm, but what was the point if he couldn't use it? His entire career would be over.

He shifted and groaned, and pain slashed through his left arm, robbing him of his breath. Was it a good thing to know he could feel pain? He forced his eyes open and stared at the heavily bandaged limb. His fingers were hugely swollen and no matter how much he tried, he couldn't move them. He concentrated on feeling them move, but no luck.

Nothing. He felt nothing.

With a disgusted sigh, he closed his eyes again, feeling guilty for the way he'd treated Rachel and Joey. They hadn't deserved his anger. He should be thanking God for saving his life, but instead he was focusing on the fact that his arm might never work right again.

Shame burned the back of his throat. He'd taught Rachel and Joey about having faith but couldn't manage to keep his own. Obviously, he owed them an apology.

But where had they gone? Now that he was awake, the pain in his arm throbbed in conjunction with the beat of his heart. His throat was still sore, no doubt from the smoke he'd inhaled out in the woods.

Abruptly, he wondered how Rachel and Joey were doing. After all, they'd inhaled a fair amount of smoke, too. Had they been checked out by a doctor? He shifted in the bed again, and a loud series of beeping noises brought a nurse running into his room.

"Relax, Mr. Butler, you need to calm down."

He almost corrected her—he was a detective, not a mister—but didn't want to waste his energy. "I need to know if Rachel and Joey Simon are both patients here, too," he croaked.

The nurse frowned down at him, as if she were worried about him. "They were here visiting you about twenty minutes ago, don't you remember?"

Twenty minutes? For some reason he thought it had been just a few minutes ago. "Are they still here?"

"I'll check for you, but you have to stay calm," the nurse said firmly. "The doctors spent a lot of time reconstructing the brachial artery in your arm. I can guarantee they won't appreciate having you damage their hard work by trying to get out of bed."

"Just find Rachel and Joey for me," he managed, not bothering to explain that he couldn't move his left arm if he tried.

The nurse left the room and it seemed like a long time before she came back carrying a small IV bag. "I have your antibiotic here," she said as she logged into the computer. "Just give me a few minutes here, okay?"

He did his best to give her the time she needed to scan his wristband and the medication, before she hung it on the IV pump. Only when she finished did he ask. "Rachel and Joey?"

"I'm sorry, but apparently they went home," she said, her tone full of sympathy.

Home? How? As far as he knew Rachel didn't have any

money or a vehicle. Had she hitched a ride with someone? Borrowed money? What?

He stared at the four walls surrounding him, feeling totally helpless. He was in no condition to follow Rachel, to make sure she and Joey were still safe. Had the police arrested Errol? He certainly hoped so. No doubt they'd be here soon to get his statement about the events that had transpired outside of Uncle Wally's cabin.

Still, he couldn't believe Rachel and Joey had left without saying goodbye.

Exhaustion weighed heavily on Rachel's shoulders as she and her son made their way back down to the hospital waiting room. She needed to figure out a way to get home, no easy feat since Chicago was about three hours from Madison. A taxi was probably out of the question, which left a bus or a train.

When she asked the woman at the front desk about a train, she shook her head. "Sorry, there's bus service to Chicago, but no train."

Of course there wasn't a train. Why would anything be easy? She was about to ask about borrowing a phone, when the police officer who'd brought her and Joey to the hospital arrived. "Ms. Simon? Could we talk for a few minutes?"

Did she really have a choice? She forced a smile, knowing that her bad mood wasn't Officer McCarthy's fault. "Sure."

"Let's talk in the chapel across the hall," the policeman suggested. "There's more privacy."

She nodded and drew Joey along with her as they crossed over to the chapel. She sank into a wooden pew and gazed at the simple yet beautifully crafted stained glass cross over the mantel. She imagined this room was used by many family members praying for their loved ones to get better.

Unfortunately, Nick didn't want her anywhere near him while he was recovering. He'd rather face his unknown future on his own.

She forced herself to push away her painful thoughts. "What can I do for you?"

"I just want to go through the events one more time," Officer McCarthy explained. "We found the dead body of Gerald Ashton, as you mentioned before. But we still haven't found the man you referred to as Dr. Karl Errol. And I have to tell you, the vehicle that was parked there is gone, too."

She shivered, hoping Karl had taken the car to parts unknown. Although certainly they could trace the car's license plates? Officer McCarthy assured her they were looking for the vehicle. So she took a deep breath and began describing the events of the night before. Midway through, Sean McCarthy interrupted, asking her to start at the beginning.

With a sigh, she went back to the night Joey was kidnapped, explaining what they'd done. The officer's expression was grim by the time she finished. "I'm not sure if that cop of yours deserves a medal or a demotion," he said. "You're lucky things didn't turn out worse."

She thought Nick definitely deserved a medal, but she didn't say anything. "Look, Officer McCarthy, Joey and I need to figure out a way to get back to Chicago."

"I can give you a ride to the bus station, if that helps," he offered.

She smiled wanly and nodded. As much as it went against the grain to ask for handouts, they'd need money for bus tickets. "Would you loan me the money for tickets? I promise I'll pay you back."

There was the slightest hesitation before he nodded. "Sure, no problem."

Relief at having one problem solved was overwhelming. "Thank you so much," she whispered.

Officer McCarthy looked uncomfortable but gave a brief nod. "Okay, let's go then. I'll come back later to get Butler's statement. He's not going anywhere soon, and I'll probably get a more coherent story once he's feeling a little better."

Thinking of Nick made her sad all over again, but she tried to hide her feelings from Joey. They followed Officer McCarthy to where he'd left his car, parked right in front of the hospital in a clear no-parking zone. The traffic around Madison was crazy busy and the ride to the bus station seemed interminable. Staring out the window to calm her frayed nerves, the Christmas decorations reminded her that the holiday was only two days away.

Inside the bus station, Officer McCarthy used his credit card to pay for their tickets, and then he handed them some cash. "Get something for you and the boy to eat," he said roughly. "And I hope you have a merry Christmas."

Tears pricked her eyes at his kindness and she'd already made a note of how much money she owed him. "Thanks again, for everything," she said softly. "And I hope you have a merry Christmas with your family, as well."

He gave both of them a nod before making his way back outside. She sank into one of the hard plastic chairs inside the bus station since the next bus didn't leave until twelve-thirty in the afternoon. Thankfully, just a few hours more and they'd be on their way home.

Waiting was the worst, but finally they boarded the bus and settled into their seats. The bus was busy with what looked like college kids heading home to their families. The ride to Chicago took much longer than she'd anticipated, partially because of the frequent stops and then because of the heavy traffic the closer they came to the city.

While they were stuck in a snarling traffic jam, Rachel realized that she didn't have her house keys. She hadn't been home since the night of Joey's kidnapping. She'd left her mangled car with the keys in it at the scene of the crash as every ounce of energy had been focused on finding her son.

With a groan, she rested her forehead on the cold glass window and realized she'd have to take a taxi to her office to pick up her spare set of keys. Yet another delay before she and Joey would finally get home.

She could hardly wait.

Nick stared at Officer McCarthy in horror. "What do you mean you didn't find Errol? And now my car is missing? Are you telling me he's still out there on the loose?" The monitor above his head sounded an alarm and he took a deep breath, trying to calm his racing heart.

"Yes. That's exactly what I'm telling you. The only body we found was Gerald Ashton's. He died of a gunshot wound to his chest."

Nick momentarily closed his eyes, feeling bad that he'd taken a life. He'd been protecting Rachel and Joey after being wounded himself. But that didn't really make him feel better.

"Where's Rachel? And Joey? We need to keep them safe in case Errol decides to come after them."

"I took them to the bus station, bought them tickets to get home and gave them a little extra cash so they could get something to eat."

"You *what?*" Nick shouted, and this time, he didn't care about the beeping alarms. He tried to throw off the covers and make his way to the side of the bed, but it wasn't easy when his left arm was wrapped up tighter than a mummy. The doctors had explained the numbness was due to some sort of pain block they'd put in, which made him feel even more like an idiot for the way he'd acted toward Rachel.

But nothing was going to stop him from doing the right thing—now.

"Mr. Butler!" his nurse cried as she came running into the room. "What are you doing?"

"It's Detective Butler," he ground out between clenched teeth, trying to ignore the sweat that beaded on his brow. "And I'm getting out of here."

"You can't leave!" The nurse looked appalled and she crossed the room to push him back into bed even as she called out for help.

Frustrated to discover he didn't have the strength of a gnat, he threw a desperate glance at McCarthy. "Help me out, here. Don't you understand? Rachel and Joey are in danger as long as Karl Errol is still on the loose! The guy is working for Global Pharmaceuticals."

"I'm calling your doctor," the nurse threatened, acting as if she hadn't heard a word he said. Or maybe she just didn't care.

"Yeah, you do that," Nick said with a disgusted sigh. "Because I'm pretty sure I have the right to leave against medical advice."

"Only if you can make it out of here without passing out cold," the nurse said tersely, holding his gaze with bold determination.

"Now, just hold on a minute," McCarthy said, holding up his hand and trying to wedge himself between Nick and the nurse. "If you really think Ms. Simon and her son are in danger, I'll help you. No need to act like a lunatic."

Nick couldn't help feeling like a lunatic. He couldn't explain the bad feeling he had about the way Rachel and

Joey had left him. Without saying goodbye. Without having Karl Errol in custody. That creep actually had his car!

"Fine," he bit out, knowing that he didn't have the strength to stay seated on the side of his bed for much longer. "What's the plan?"

"How about if I send some backup out to meet Ms. Simon and her son at the Chicago bus depot," McCarthy offered. "They can drive her home, stick around a bit to make sure everything's all right."

It was a start, but not good enough. "We need to get to Chicago, ASAP. I need you to help me get out of here," he said to McCarthy. "I'll need help since I can barely keep myself upright. We need to get to Rachel before Errol does."

"I don't know if that's a good idea," McCarthy hedged.

"I do. Trust me—I'll take full responsibility for my decision." Last year, Jonah had been in a similar situation, leaving the hospital against doctor's orders. And he'd been fine.

Nick had to believe everything would work out fine this time, too.

Dear Lord, please give me the strength I need to keep Rachel and Joey safe.

Rachel held on to Joey's hand tightly as they navigated the crowds at the bus depot. Without luggage, it was easy to push her way through the swarming mass of people to the door, and before long they found their way to the taxi stand. Now that they were back in Chicago, she couldn't wait to get home. But first a quick trip to her office building.

Her desperation must have shown as a taxi came barreling to a stop right in front of her. She thought she heard someone call her name but then figured she was imagining things. She urged Joey in first and climbed in after him.

"Where to?" the cabbie asked in a thick Middle Eastern accent.

"Simon Incorporated," she told him, rattling off the address. He nodded and pulled out into traffic, earning a loud protest from the guy behind him.

She almost closed her eyes, because the taxi drivers in Chicago were maniacs behind the wheel, and she always expected to get in a crash. But somehow, miraculously, they always managed to get to their destinations unscathed.

"Are we home yet?" Joey asked plaintively. She knew he was exhausted, and he'd truly taken everything in stride better than she could have expected.

"Almost. We're going to stop by my office first, so I can pay the taxi driver and get our house keys," she said in a hushed voice, hoping the driver didn't understand English very well. She didn't think he'd have agreed to take her anywhere knowing that she didn't have anything more than ten dollars in her pocket, courtesy of Officer McCarthy's donation. She intended to get a check in the mail to him first thing in the morning, thanking him again for helping her out.

Joey sighed heavily but didn't whine or complain.

The traffic worked against them again, and she kept a wary eye on the time, hoping they'd get there before the office building shut down for the day. It was almost five o'clock in the evening and already pitch-black outside, except for the brightly lit buildings and the various Christmas decorations, of course.

She chewed her lower lip nervously. Hopefully, even if everyone was gone, the security guards would let her upstairs. Maybe Gerry hadn't had time to completely take over her company. Just the thought of explaining how Gerry had died was enough to overwhelm her.

It was five-fifteen when the taxi driver pulled up in front of her building. "Keep the meter running...I'll be right back."

"No! You pay first!" he protested.

"Look, I promise you I'll be back. We need to get home. I don't have a car."

He stared at her with eyes black as midnight but then he nodded. "If you not back soon, I come after you."

She breathed a tiny sigh of relief. "I will, I promise." Sliding out from the backseat, she waited for Joey to join her and headed inside.

Carrie, the perky receptionist, left promptly at five, but there was a security guard seated in her spot. Being inside the office building after being gone for so long seemed a little strange yet, at the same time, blessedly familiar. "George, how are you? How are the kids?"

"Great, Ms. Simon, just great. What are you doing here so late?"

"I forgot something up in my office. Would you mind letting me use the master key?" She hoped and prayed that Gerry hadn't told everyone to keep her out of the building.

"Sure, no problem." George held out a key. "Just bring it back when you leave."

"I will." She didn't hesitate, but went straight over to the bank of elevators. The doors opened immediately, taking them all the way to the tenth floor without a single stop.

She unlocked the door, noting that the entire office area was completely dark, as if everyone had gone home early. And considering it was nearly Christmas, she understood why. She flipped on lights as she walked down the hall to her office.

Her door stood open, which she thought was a little odd. Edith always kept the door closed and locked when Rachel wasn't there. Then again, the woman had given her notice. For all she knew, Edith hadn't even shown up for work today.

Hovering in the doorway, she reached inside to flip on the lights. She blinked for a moment so that her eyes could adjust before crossing the room to her desk and rummaging for cash and her keys. Joey plopped into her desk chair, spinning from side to side.

She was relieved to find her secret stash of bills was right where she'd left it. She grabbed the money and the spare set of keys.

"I've been waiting for you, Rachel."

The voice came from the hallway, and she swallowed a scream when she jerked her head up to see Karl Errol standing in the shadows. Her heart dropped to her stomach when she realized he'd traded the rifle for a small hand-gun, which he pointed directly at her. From this distance it would be hard for him to miss.

"Karl!" She faced him in the doorway, making sure to keep Joey behind her, hoping her son would figure out a way to slide down behind the desk. All the while, she kept her eyes locked on the research scientist. She couldn't believe Karl was here. How did he know that she'd stop by on her way home? Or had he planned to wait for her all night, surprising her in the morning? She swallowed hard, wishing she'd asked George to come up with her.

How long did she have to stall here before the cabbie came looking for his money? Or would he simply give up and drive away? She tried not to think the worst. "I'm so glad you're all right. We looked everywhere for you!"

"Yeah, right. You left me there to die, Rachel," he

sneered with obvious reproach. "Good thing I still had the distributer cap for the car, hmm?"

"What do you want, Karl?" she asked, fed up with pandering to his ego. "What more could you possibly want from me?"

"I need to finish what I started," he said enigmatically. "I always finish the job."

"Why?" she asked helplessly, tired of the games. "Haven't you caused enough damage? You've ruined my company's reputation, and for what? Love? You don't have the faintest idea what true love is. Josie never would have accepted your love if she knew what you've done."

She couldn't help thinking of Nick. How she'd left him in the hospital without even giving him a chance to explain what he'd gone through. Maybe he had shut her out, believing the worst about the damage to his arm, but sooner or later, he would have come around. If she'd learned anything about faith, it was that leaning on God's strength could help you through the darkest days. She was suddenly ashamed of her actions. She should have stayed. She should have given him a second chance.

Should have told him how she felt.

Now she could only hope and pray she wasn't too late.

"Do you honestly think that Detective Butler won't figure out that you're the one who killed me?" she continued, since Karl hadn't responded. "He's not stupid, Karl. I promise Nick won't rest until he finds you and makes sure that you spend the rest of your life behind bars."

"I have protection. My boss will protect me."

"Protection? From your boss? William Hanson, the CEO of Global? Or the Mafia?"

The way Karl reacted to William Hanson's name let her know she'd nailed it correctly. For once she didn't mind being wrong about the Mafia connection.

"You think William Hanson cares about you? I'm betting that as soon as you kill me, he'll do whatever it takes to get rid of you."

Karl scowled. "He won't kill me—I helped him out. He's already beaten you to market with a new diabetes drug. One that doesn't cause blood clots."

The thought of Karl purposefully ruining the new medication she'd put out to market made her seethe with anger. Not just because of her company's reputation, but because of the innocent people he'd hurt.

"So why kill me if Global has the new medication out?"

"My boss doesn't like loose ends. And since Ashton couldn't manage to do my dirty work for me, I have no choice but to finish this on my own."

Her heart leaped into her throat when he lifted the gun. "No matter what you do to me, Nick won't stop searching for you. I've already told the police about you, too. You'll never be safe, Karl."

Karl didn't answer; instead, he simply stared at her as if he hadn't heard a word she'd said. She had no way of knowing if she'd even gotten through to him.

She tried not to panic. Facing a crazy man with a gun was much harder when she didn't have Nick's reassuring presence nearby. But she'd left Nick back at the hospital in Madison.

She and Joey were on their own.

SEVENTEEN

Nick dozed during the long ride back to Chicago. Even with Sean McCarthy using flashing red lights and sirens, the trip took longer than he wanted. The doctor back in Madison had been really angry about him leaving, but he couldn't worry about his arm.

Rachel and Joey were far more important.

They swung by Rachel's house, which thankfully wasn't that far from her office building, but the place was locked up tight with no sign of anyone having been there. He told Sean to head over to the office building next, figuring that Rachel probably needed her keys.

When they reached the office complex, Sean parked behind a taxi with the "in service" light on. Nick managed to get out of the passenger seat under his own power, holding his left arm protectively against his body to minimize the pain as much as possible. Now that the numbing agent had worn off, he could feel his arm, but mostly all he felt was pain.

When they walked into the building there was a foreign taxi driver yelling at the security guard behind the desk. Nick couldn't understand half of what the guy was saying, but it became apparent that the taxi driver had brought Rachel and Joey here and wanted his money.

"Pay the man," he told Sean, before turning his attention back to the security guard who wore a name tag with the name George. He didn't know if that was a first name or a last name. "Are Rachel and Joey Simon upstairs in her office?" he asked.

"Yes, they went up about five minutes ago," the security guard said.

"Did anyone else go up either before or after her?" Sean asked, after paying the taxi driver.

"I've only been here about twenty minutes, but no one else went up while I was here." George cast a curious glance between Sean and Nick. "Is something wrong?"

"We don't know for sure," Nick said. "But we're heading up right now to make sure she's all right. If we don't come back down within ten minutes, call the police."

"Maybe I should go with you?" George offered.

"No, you need to stay here," Nick told him. "Make sure no one else goes up, do you understand?"

George nodded. "Got it."

Sean had already made his way over to the one of the six banks of elevators, and he was holding the door, waiting for Nick. He fought a wave of dizziness as he hurried in.

The ride to the tenth floor was quick and when the doors opened, the ding of the elevator seemed exceptionally loud. He hoped no one had overheard it.

"Stay back," Sean warned in a whisper, as he made his way into Rachel's office suite.

Nick had his weapon tucked into the waistband of his jeans but was hampered by the need to hold his left arm still, so he nodded, knowing that he would only be a liability if he didn't give Sean the room he needed.

The moment they opened the glass doors to the office area, Nick heard talking. And from the way Rachel was pleading with someone, he suspected Karl was there.

He couldn't see much with Sean in front of him, but the hint of desperation in her tone wrenched his heart. It was his fault she was here with Joey. If he'd responded differently in the hospital she probably would have stayed.

Especially if he'd had asked her to stay.

Please, Lord, keep Rachel and Joey safe!

Rachel saw something move behind Karl's right shoulder, but she did her best to keep her gaze trained on his so that he wouldn't figure it out.

"Karl, please. Give me the gun. I can tell you're not a cold-blooded killer," she said, stalling for time. She couldn't tell who was creeping up behind Karl, but just knowing she and Joey weren't alone was enough to give her hope and strength.

Besides, she was getting mighty tired of people pointing guns at her.

"Stay back or I'll shoot," Karl threatened, although the gun in his hand wavered just a bit.

"You want money, Karl?" she asked. "Because if that's the case then I'll double their fee if you'll put the gun down. I'll give you enough to change your name and leave town. Think about it—you'll get a fresh start."

Surprisingly, he seemed to consider her offer. But just as he was about to speak, an arm came around from behind and snatched the gun from his grasp.

"What the—" Karl's sentence was cut off when he was slammed up against the wall, Sean McCarthy's arm planted firmly across his neck.

Rachel sagged against the edge of her desk in relief. She'd never been so happy to see a cop in her life. She didn't know how Sean had gotten here from Madison so fast, but she was thankful just the same.

"Karl Errol, you're under arrest for attempted murder and corporate espionage, and anything else that you've done that I haven't figured out yet," Sean McCarthy said, pulling out his handcuffs and clasping them firmly over Errol's wrists. The way the research scientist sagged against the door convinced her that he'd finally given up.

Thank You, Lord.

"Rachel? Are you and Joey all right?"

She straightened and looked past Sean into the hall-way, tempted to pinch herself in the arm to make sure that she wasn't imagining Nick standing there. "Nick? Is that really you?"

After making sure Joey was okay, she found herself staring at Nick, unable to look away. He was propped against the wall, holding his left arm against him, his mouth bracketed with pain.

"Yeah. I had to make sure you and Joey were all right," he said.

She was so glad to see him, even though it was obvi-ous he shouldn't be here. "What were you thinking?" she scolded as she rushed forward to meet him. "You should have stayed in the hospital. What if you lose the circula-tion in your arm?"

"It's nothing compared to the thought of losing you," he murmured, holding her gaze with his. "I'm sorry I hurt you, Rachel. I didn't mean to. I never should have allowed my faith to waver."

Her heart melted at his words, and she would have engulfed him in a huge hug if not for the fact that Nick looked as if he was hanging on by a thread. His brow was damp with sweat and his face was pale, two indications that he absolutely should not have left the hospital.

"Nick!" Joey cried as he ran forward, putting his arms around Nick's waist and hugging him hard. She caught the wince on Nick's features, but he didn't protest. "You're here!"

"Yeah, I'm here, buddy."

"Are you all better now?" Joey asked, tipping his head back to look up at Nick.

"Not exactly..." Nick said drily.

"Not at all," Rachel interjected with a deep frown. "You need to get back to Madison, Nick. The surgeon told me that the first twenty-four hours are critical. It's barely been twelve hours since surgery and a good portion of that had to be traveling here."

"Maybe you're right," he said, and the fact that he didn't try to argue with her was worrisome.

Before she could say anything more, he let go of Joey and slid down the wall to the floor.

"I told him to stay behind, but did he listen? No, he didn't." Sean's tone held disgust. "I guess we'd better call 911, the only way he's getting out of here is in an ambulance."

"I've already called 911," George said, coming down the hall toward them. "You made me nervous, and when you didn't come down right away, I decided to make the call. Good thing I did. The cops should be here any minute."

"Make sure there's an ambulance, too, would you, George?" she asked. She'd sat down on the floor beside Nick, holding his head in her lap, unwilling to let him go, even for a minute.

"That surgeon is going to say 'I told you so,'" Sean joked, as he stared down at Nick's prone figure.

"Was worth it," Nick murmured in a voice so soft Rachel was sure she was the only one who could hear him.

"Rest now, Nick," she said, smoothing her fingers down his rough, bristly cheek. "We're safe now...."

There was a lot of commotion when the police arrived and soon after an ambulance crew showed up carrying a gurney.

She thought Nick was out cold, but suddenly his eyes opened and he reached for her hand. "Come with me to the hospital," he said hoarsely.

"I'll meet you there," she promised. "Just do what the doctor says this time, okay?"

Grimacing, he nodded his head. Then she slid out of the way, allowing the paramedics to lift Nick onto the gurney.

And for the second time in less than twenty-four hours, she stood with her arm around Joey, watching as the paramedics wheeled away the man she loved.

After Sean had handed Karl over to the Chicago authorities and she'd once again given her statement to the police, she convinced Sean to take her and Joey home.

Once there, she gave him the money she owed him, even though he kept trying to wave it away.

"Please take the money," she begged. "You've already done so much for me and my son. Please?"

Sean reluctantly took the cash. "Do you want me to drive you to the hospital before I head home?" he asked gruffly.

She hesitated but then shook her head. "No, we can take a cab or the subway. Getting around Chicago is much easier than trying to get around in Madison," she teased.

"Hey, I live out in the boondocks, so this is all new to me," the officer said with a wry grin. "We don't get this kind of big-city crime where I come from."

Her smile faded. "Be glad, Sean. Be very glad."

He slung his arm across her shoulder in a friendly

hug. "Don't worry, this was enough excitement to last me quite a while."

After he left, she decided to take a shower before heading back to the hospital. She urged Joey to take one, too.

Freshly scrubbed and wearing clean clothing made her feel like a new person, although it was clear her son was still exhausted. She was tired, too, but she wanted to see Nick in the hospital, one more time, before they came home to sleep.

And even though she knew she could call a babysitter to stay home with Joey, she preferred to keep him with her, despite being certain the danger was finally over.

Besides, she figured Joey would feel better, knowing firsthand that Nick was going to be all right.

When they arrived at Chicago North Hospital, they found Nick was a patient in a regular room rather than being back in the ICU. They walked into his room just as a voice announced through the overhead speaker that visiting hours would be over in fifteen minutes.

"Hey, how are you feeling?" she asked, crossing over to Nick's bed. Joey stood at the foot of Nick's bed, regarding him thoughtfully.

"My ears are blistered from having the doctors yell at me for fifteen minutes straight, but otherwise I'm good." His expression was more relaxed, and the brackets around his mouth had vanished, which she assumed meant he'd been given some pain medication.

"You look much better," she murmured. "And you deserve to have your ears blistered after that stunt you pulled."

"They wanted to transport me back to Madison General, but I guess the doctor there wasn't too interested in having me back." A hint of a smile played along the corner of his mouth. "Can't say that I blame him."

"How's the circulation in your arm?" she asked, glancing at the limb that was currently propped up on two pillows.

He moved his fingers and shrugged his right shoulder. "Pretty good, I guess. I can move my hand a bit more. No harm done, at least according to the surgeon here. I think that's one of the reasons he didn't push the issue of sending me back. Apparently, surgeons don't like to pick up other surgeon's leftovers."

She laughed, extremely relieved to hear that Nick wasn't any worse for wear.

"How long will you have to stay in the hospital, Nick?" Joey asked anxiously.

"Shouldn't be more than a day or two," Nick responded.

Joey's expression clouded. "But that means you'll be in here over Christmas."

"That's okay," Nick said quickly. "I don't mind."

There was another overhead announcement instructing all visitors to leave the building, so Rachel reached over and took Nick's good hand in hers, squeezing gently. "We'd better get home. I promised Joey that he would be able to sleep in his own bed tonight."

"All right." Nick's eyes were at half-mast and she suspected that he'd be asleep before they made it out the front door.

"See you tomorrow," she promised, releasing his hand. "Come on, Joey. Let's go home."

"Bye, Nick." Joey flashed a grin before following her out of the room.

As they left the hospital to flag down a cab, she decided that since Nick was going to be in the hospital for Christmas, they would need to bring Christmas to him.

Nick hated being stuck in the hospital. The only bright spot in his day was that his arm seemed to be doing better. The doctors had taken down the bulky dressing to examine the incision and hadn't put it back on, making him feel ten pounds lighter.

"Looks better than it should," the surgeon told him grudgingly. "Considering you went several hours without your blood-thinning medicine, you're extremely lucky."

"I'm blessed," Nick corrected with a grin. "Truly blessed." He'd slept on and off during the night, waking up between pain medication doses, but he'd had plenty of time to think about what had happened up at the cabin. How much he'd wanted to live, when he'd managed to convince himself that he'd be happy for God to call him home. After missing his wife and daughter for so long, he realized that God meant for him to move on with his life. He wasn't sure what he'd done to deserve a second chance, but he couldn't deny the way Rachel and Joey had wiggled their way into his heart.

Now, if he could only find a way to convince Rachel to take a chance on him.

Outside his window, he noticed snow was beginning to fall. He wondered if that change in the weather was part of the reason that Rachel and Joey hadn't come in to visit him yet.

He couldn't bear to think that maybe they wouldn't show at all. Rachel had said she'd see him tomorrow. Surely she wouldn't have said that if she hadn't meant it.

But when the lunch hour came and went he began to lose hope. He exercised his fingers the way he was supposed to and wondered if he could convince Jonah or someone from the precinct to bust him out of here again.

If she didn't show up soon, he'd have no choice but to go to her.

"Knock-knock," a voice said from the doorway. Relief flooded him when he realized that Rachel and Joey had arrived.

"Come in," he called, struggling to sit farther up in his bed. He was tired of looking and feeling like an invalid.

The first thing he saw was a small pine tree about three feet tall covering most of Joey's face. His smile widened when he saw Rachel coming in behind the boy, lugging a large bag.

"Merry Christmas," she said as Joey set the small pine tree on the bedside table.

"Merry Christmas," he responded, unable to suppress his broad grin. It was after all, Christmas Eve.

"Close your eyes," she said, as she plunked the bag down on the guest chair. "We'll tell you when you can open them again."

He'd rather have gazed at Rachel all day but did as she requested. He could hear Joey giggling amidst the sounds of paper rustling. With his eyes closed, he could smell the refreshing scent of pine from the small tree.

It seemed like forever, but finally the rustling and the giggling stopped. "You can open your eyes now, Nick," Joey said excitedly.

He opened his eyes and gasped in surprise at the way they'd transformed his room. Not only was the tiny tree decorated with miniature lights, but there was a small nativity scene set out on display along with several strands of garland strung festively around the whiteboard on the wall.

"Beautiful," he murmured, and he wasn't talking about the Christmas decorations.

Rachel looked lovely, no doubt in part because she'd finally gotten a decent night's sleep. Her smile was shy and it took him a minute to realize she had what looked to be a brand-new Bible in her hands.

"I hope you don't mind, but I thought we could read the Christmas story again tonight," she said. "Or we could read the Psalms since I know you mentioned they're your favorite. I read Psalm 23 this morning and I can certainly understand why you like them so much. I feel blessed to have found God. And I owe it all to you."

His throat was tight with pent up emotion and he had to clear it before he could speak. "I'd like that," he managed, keeping his gaze centered on her. "Very much."

"I, um, didn't know how to get in touch with your family, so they don't know that you've been injured...."

"Rachel, come here," he said, holding out his good hand.

She approached him and put her hand in his. He was conscious of Joey watching them curiously so he couldn't say exactly what he wanted, but she needed to know the truth. "I'm happy just having you and Joey here, and I don't need anyone else."

Her gaze was uncertain. "Are you sure? Christmas is a time for families."

"I'm sure." He lifted her hand and kissed it, wishing that Joey wasn't there so he could kiss her properly. "You and Joey are all the family I need."

She blushed but didn't pull her hand away. "I'm glad," she murmured.

And it wasn't until much later, when Joey had fallen asleep in the chair, that he was able to tell Rachel how he felt.

"I'm falling in love with you, Rachel," he said softly.

She sucked in a quick breath. "How can you be so sure?"

He tried to think of a way to put his feelings into words. "I thought I was happy, living my life alone, doing my best to put the bad guys behind bars. But when you and

Joey came into my life, I realized that I never felt as alive as I did with the both of you."

Her eyes glistened with tears. "I've been so afraid to get involved with anyone after Anthony. I told myself that I was protecting Joey, but I think in reality, I was protecting myself."

He took her hand and drew her closer. "Rachel, give me a chance to show you how much I love you. There's no rush, you can take all the time you need, if you'll just give me a chance."

"All right," she whispered.

"Is that a yes?" Nick asked, needing to hear her say the words.

She smiled and leaned over to kiss him, which was perfect since he wasn't able to get up and cross over to her thanks to the IV pumps keeping him tied to the bed. "That's a big yes, Nick. Because I've fallen in love with you, too."

He grinned, wishing she'd kiss him again, hardly able to believe his good fortune. Or rather, maybe he could.

For God had known the path he should take, all along.

EPILOGUE

Three months later...

Nick paused outside Rachel's doorway, patting the pocket that held the ring he'd purchased for her as he tried to quell his nerves.

He'd gone back to work last week, although he was still on desk duty thanks to his arm injury. He was grateful that each week his arm strength seemed to get a little better, so he didn't complain. Turns out there really wasn't any Mafia connection to Global Pharmaceuticals. Just a greedy CEO who'd hated Rachel's father. When Karl had implicated him in the espionage related to the defective diabetes drug, he'd crumpled like a house of cards.

Rachel and Joey's nightmare was truly over.

As glad as Nick was to know they were safe, getting back into the normal routine of doing investigations had cut into the time he'd been able to spend with Rachel and Joey.

Especially Rachel.

Last night, he'd picked up Joey after his last basketball game and had asked the boy's permission to marry his mom. Joey had been thrilled and Nick could only hope that the youngster had managed to keep his secret.

He pushed the doorbell, listening to the chimes echo through the house. He was pleasantly surprised when Rachel opened the door. "Hi, Nick."

"Hi, Rachel." He drew her in for a long kiss. "I've missed you," he murmured, gazing down at her upturned face.

"I missed you, too," she said with a smile. "Are you ready to go?"

"Sure. Is, uh, Joey around?"

"Yes, he's decided to have a friend sleep over tonight. Suzy, the babysitter, doesn't seem to mind."

Nick grinned. "Just give me a minute to say hello."

"All right," she agreed, standing back so he could come inside. The boys were sprawled in front of the television in the living room, playing some sort of basketball video game. Suzy was sitting with earbuds in place, listening to music.

"Hey, Joey, how are you?" Nick greeted him.

"Pause the game," Joey said to his friend, as he jumped off the sofa. "Hi, Nick!"

Nick bent his head down to Joey's. "Did you keep our secret?" he asked.

Joey's eyes gleamed as he nodded. "Yep."

"Good." He relaxed a bit. "Thanks, buddy. Now try not to interrupt us at dinner, okay?"

Joey rolled his eyes. "Why would I? Suzy is here. Besides, me and Ben are going to be busy playing our game, anyway."

"All right, see you later, then."

"Suzy, text me if you need anything," Rachel called out as he returned to her.

"Don't worry, we'll be fine," Suzy responded.

Nick drove Rachel to the small Italian restaurant where

he'd reserved a private table in the corner. "How was work today?" he asked.

"The lawsuit has been settled and the new researchers seem to be doing all right so far." Rachel's smile dimmed. "The company will be on shaky financial ground for a while, but we'll make it."

"I know you will," Nick replied, admiring her determination. He pulled into the parking lot and handed his keys to the valet service before escorting Rachel inside.

"My favorite restaurant." Rachel beamed as they were seated. "I already know what I'm having."

"You should, since you have the menu memorized." He waited until the server had taken their order before reaching across the table to take her hand. "Rachel, these past few months with you have been wonderful."

She smiled and squeezed his hand. "For me, too, Nick."

The timing seemed right, so he took a deep breath and rose to his feet. Two steps brought him to Rachel's side and when he went down on one knee, her eyes rounded and her mouth formed a small O.

"Nick?" she whispered, looking a bit like she was in shock.

He smiled gently as he pulled the ring box out of his pocket and opened it. "Rachel, Joey has already given me his blessing. He told me he'd be thrilled to have me as his dad. So now it's up to you."

Her eyes filled with tears and for a moment he almost panicked, until he saw the tremulous smile bloom across her face. "I love you, Rachel. Will you please marry me?"

She barely looked at the ring, instead holding his gaze with hers. "Yes, Nick. I'd love nothing more than to be your wife. And to have you be Joey's father. Of course, I'll marry you."

Yes! He did a mental fist pump but managed to draw

her to her feet so that he could kiss her. He held her tight, wishing he never had to let her go.

The entire restaurant erupted into a round of applause.

He had to chuckle as he pulled away. "I love you, Rachel. And I promise to make you happy," he vowed.

She tilted her head to the side, her gaze solemn. "I love you, Nick, and I promise to make you happy, too."

He didn't doubt the sincerity in her tone for a moment and knew that he was doubly blessed to have found true love for the second time.

* * * * *

Dear Reader,

You may remember Detective Nick Butler from my most recent story *Undercover Cowboy*. Once I finished writing Logan and Kate's romance, I decided I couldn't leave poor Nick hanging out there without a story of his own.

Rachel Simon is the CEO of Simon Inc., but when her nine-year-old son, Joey, is kidnapped right from under her nose, she's willing to give up everything she owns to get him back safely. Especially when she fears the Mafia might be the mastermind behind the kidnapping.

Detective Nick Butler lost his own wife and young daughter several years ago, so he understands the angst Rachel is going through. But while he's willing to do whatever is necessary to help her get Joey back, he's determined not to let anyone replace his wife and daughter in his heart.

Working together to stay safe, Rachel and Nick both slowly learn to trust each other. Can they also open their hearts and their minds to the possibility of love?

I hope you enjoy reading Rachel and Nick's story. I'm always thrilled and honored to hear from my readers and I can be reached through my website at www.laurascott-books.com.

Yours in faith,
Laura Scott

Questions for Discussion

1. In the beginning of the story, Joey is kidnapped and Rachel is beside herself. Discuss a time when you felt the same sense of despair and hopelessness.

2. In question number one above, discuss how different Rachel may have felt if she'd had faith in the beginning of the story.

3. As Rachel and Nick search for Joey, Rachel begins to pray. Discuss a time when you first began to pray and learned how to lean on God's strength.

4. Once Joey has been freed from his kidnappers, Rachel is worried about her son becoming too attached to Nick. Do you think her fears are warranted? Why or why not?

5. Rachel feels guilty when she hears Joey say he wished he knew God was always with him, because then he wouldn't have felt so alone. Discuss a time when you felt alone and had to lean on your faith.

6. While Rachel and Nick are in the cabin, Rachel finds the Bible and begins to read. Discuss the first time you began reading the Bible and how that experience impacted your faith.

7. Nick reads the story of Christmas from the Bible. Discuss and share your favorite Christmas tradition.

8. When Nick has been injured, he thinks God is calling him home and he isn't quite ready to go. Discuss

whether or not you might feel the same way in a similar circumstance.

9. After Nick is in the hospital, he can't feel his arm and he has a brief moment where he loses his faith. Discuss a time when you had a similar experience.

10. Toward the end of the story, Rachel realizes she gave up on Nick too soon when she left him in the hospital to go home. Discuss a time when you were upset with someone you loved and how you overcame your feelings.

REQUEST YOUR FREE BOOKS!

2 FREE RIVETING INSPIRATIONAL NOVELS
PLUS 2 FREE MYSTERY GIFTS

Love Inspired
SUSPENSE
RIVETING INSPIRATIONAL ROMANCE

Pulled from the waves and gasping for air, the last person
Antonia Verde expects to be her rescuer is Rueben Sandoval.
He may once have been the love of her life, but his
drug-smuggling brother ruined their chance of happiness.
Now with a storm blowing in, Rueben's island hotel is her only
refuge. Soon they find themselves trapped on the island with a
killer in the midst of a dangerous hurricane. Antonia's life is in
Rueben's hands—can she trust him with her heart, as well?

Stormswept

FORCE OF NATURE
by
DANA MENTINK

*is available December 2013 wherever
Love Inspired Suspense books are sold.*

Christmas has a way of reminding us of what really matters—and what
could be more important than our loved ones? From husbands and wives
to boyfriends and girlfriends to long-lost loves, the real-life romances in this
book are surrounded by the joy and blessings of the Christmas season.

Featuring stories by favorite Love Inspired authors, this collection
will warm your heart and soothe your soul through the long winter.
A Kiss Under the Mistletoe beautifully celebrates the way love and faith can
transform a cold day in December into the most magical day of the year.

On sale now!

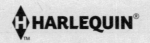

*Bygones's intrepid reporter is on the trail of the town's
mysterious benefactor. Will she succeed in her mission?*

Read on for a preview of
COZY CHRISTMAS
by Valerie Hansen, the conclusion to
THE HEART OF MAIN STREET *series.*

Whitney Leigh rolled her eyes. "Romance! It's getting to
be an epidemic."

Because she was alone in the car, she didn't try to temper her frustration. Fortunately, this time, the editor of the
Bygones Gazette had assigned her to write a new series
about the Save Our Streets project's six-month anniversary.
If he had asked her for one more fluff piece on recent
engagements, she would have screamed.

Parking in front of the Cozy Cup Café, she shivered and
slid out.

As a lifelong citizen of Bygones, she was supposed to
have been perfect for the job of ferreting out the hidden
facts concerning the town's windfall. Too bad she had failed.
Instead of an exposé, she'd ended up filling her column
with news of people's love lives. But she was not going to
quit investigating. No, sir. Not until she'd uncovered the
real facts. Especially the name of their secret benefactor.

She stepped inside the Cozy Cup.

"What can I do for you?" Josh Smith asked.

Whitney was tempted to launch right into her real reason
for being there. Instead, she merely said, "Fix me something warm?"

"Like what?"

"Surprise me."

She settled herself at one of the tables. There was something unique about this place. And, truth to tell, the same went for the other new businesses on Main. Each one had filled a need and become an integral part of Bygones in a mere five or six months.

Josh Smith was a prime example. He was what she considered young, yet he had quickly won over the older generations as well as the younger ones.

He stepped out from behind the counter with a steaming cup in one hand and a taller, whipped-cream-topped tumbler in the other.

"Your choice," he said pleasantly, placing both drinks on the table and joining her as if he already knew this was not a social call.

"I see you're not too busy this afternoon. Do you have time to talk?"

"I always have time for my favorite reporter," he said.

"How many reporters do you know?"

"Hmm, let's see." A widening grin made his eyes sparkle. "One."

Will Whitney get her story and find love in the process?

Pick up COZY CHRISTMAS to find out.
Available December 2013
wherever Love Inspired® Books are sold.